This book is to be returned on or before
the last date stamped below

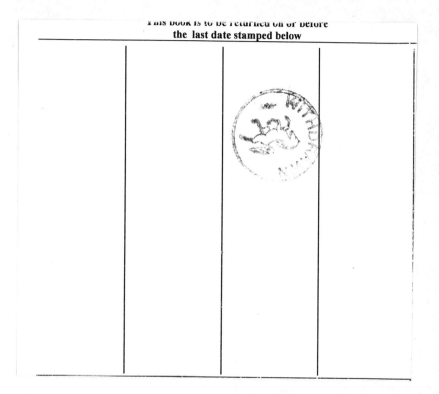

*To Ma Kringle, who made this book possible,
and to all the hard-working women
of the world who try their utmost to make
Christmas a very special occasion.*

Christine Kringle

Lynn Brittney

Illustrations by Brita Granström

Design and typography Kate Lowe

www.christinekringle.com

THE YULE DYNASTY

Who they are and what they are called:

Argentina
Gift Bringers ~ *The Three Kings*

Armenia
Gift Bringer ~ *Gaghant Baba*

Australia
Gift Bringer ~ *Santa (aka OzNick)*

Austria
Gift Bringer ~ *Niklo*

Azerbaijani
Gift Bringer ~ *Shakta Babah*

Belgium
Gift Bringer ~ *St.Nicholas*
Helper ~ *Black Pete*

Brazil
Gift Bringer ~ *Papai Noel*

Bulgaria
Gift Bringer ~ *Diado Coleda*

Canada
Gift Bringer ~ *Belsnickle*
Female Gift Bringer (French Canada) ~ *Tante Arie*

China
Gift Bringer ~ *Dun Che Lao Ren (aka Christmas Old Man)*

Czech Republic
Gift Bringer ~ *St.Nicholas*
Helper ~ *Cert*

Denmark
Gift Bringer ~ *Julemanden*

Finland
Gift Bringer ~ *Old Man Christmas*

France
Gift Bringer ~ *Pere Noel*
Female Gift Bringer ~ *Tante Arie*

Germany
Gift Bringer ~ *Der Weinachtsmann*
Helpers (depending upon the region) ~
Knecht Ruprecht, Krampus, Hans Muff
Pelzebock, Gumphinkel

Ghana
Gift Bringer ~ *Father Christmas*
Greece
Gift Bringer ~ *Hagios Nikolaos*
Hawaii
Gift Bringer ~ *Kanakaloka*

Holland
Gift Bringer ~ *Sinterklaas*
Helper ~ *Black Peter*
Hungary
Gift Bringer ~ *Santa Claus*
Ireland
Gift Bringer ~ *Santy Claus*
Iceland
Gift Bringers ~ *9 Jole Sveinars –*
Bowl Licker
Door Slammer
Window Peeper
Candle Beggar
Yogurt Slurper
Shortie
Spoon Licker
Sausage Hooker
Meat Hooker
Italy
Gift Bringer ~ *Babbo Natale*
Female Gift Bringer ~ *La Befana*
Japan
Gift Bringer ~ *Santa Kurohsu*
Latvia
Gift Bringer ~ *Winter Holiday Man*
Lithuania
Gift Bringer ~ *Kaledu Senis*
Luxembourg
Gift Bringer ~ *St.Nicholas*
Mexico
Gift Bringer ~ *The Three Kings*
Helper ~ *Black Pete*
New Zealand
Gift Bringer ~ *Father Christmas*

Norway
Gift Bringer ~ *Julenisse*
Peru
Gift Bringer ~ *Papai Noel*
Poland
Gift Bringer ~ *The Star Man*
Portugal
Gift Bringer ~ *Pia Natal*
Puerto Rico
Gift Bringers ~ *The Three Kings*
Russia
Gift Bringer ~ *Grandfather Frost*
Female Gift Bringer ~ *Babushka*
Serbo-Croatia
Gift Bringer ~ *Bozic Bata*
Sicily
Female Gift Bringer ~ *Santa Lucia*
Spain
Gift Bringers ~ *The Three Kings*
Papa Noel
Slovakia
Gift Bringer ~ *St Mikulas*
Sweden
Gift Bringer ~ *Jultomten*
Female Gift Bringer ~ *St.Lucia*
Switzerland
Gift Bringer ~ *Samichlaus*
Female Gift Bringer ~ *St.Lucy*
Helper ~ *Schmutzli*
Turkey
Gift Bringer ~ *St.Nick*
Ukraine
Gift Bringer ~ *Bishop Nicholas*
United Kingdom (England, Scotland, Wales and N. Ireland)
Gift Bringer ~ *Santa Claus (aka Father Christmas)*
Uruguay
Gift Bringer ~ *Feliz Navidad*
USA
Gift Bringer ~ *Kriss Kringle (aka Santa Claus)*
Venezuela
Gift Bringer ~ *San Nicolas*

CONTENTS

CHAPTER ONE

The Conference

The popular myth, that most people choose to believe, is that there is only one Santa Claus – an immortal being who brings presents to all the children of the world in one night. The reality, as anyone who is a member of the Yule Dynasty knows, is that there are, actually, many, many Santas – all with different names, all servicing their own countries or regions – and they are not immortal at all.

Granted, the average male life expectancy of a Yule is around 270 years but these Santa's operate family businesses (or, as Der Wiehnachtsmann of Germany prefers to call it – "franchises" – so firm is his family's belief that they were the first and all others came after) and the job is handed down from father to son.

This, in essence, was the problem that was facing the Kringle family, the USA branch of the Yule Dynasty, as they flew towards the final approach of Korvatunturi Reindeerport in Finland for the annual Yule Conference. Kriss Kringle, one the busiest and most hardworking members of the Yule Dynasty, due to the large population of the United States, had no male heir. He and Mrs Kringle had been blessed only with a daughter, Christine, who was now fourteen years old.

It was time, as Ma Kringle had said, before they left home, "to bite the bullet." This year, Kriss was going to propose a motion that females be allowed to inherit the mantle of Christmas Gift Bringer. He knew it would be unpopular, particularly with the Italian and

Russian branches of the family, who had spent several centuries fighting a rearguard action against the female Gift Bringers of their own culture.

Babbo Natale of Italy was continually irked by the competition from La Befana, the old woman who, so the legend goes, followed the Three Wise Men to Bethlehem. Unfortunately, she missed the baby Jesus, so an angel gave her the job of giving presents to children each year.

Grandfather Frost of Russia had had an easier time of it during the years of the Communist regime in the USSR. Their version of La Befana – Babushka – had been banned, due to her religious links, but now that Russia and the other Slavonic countries had rediscovered religion, Babushka had come back with a vengeance. So much so, that she had even organized a breakaway conference of Female Gift Bringers last year called, *Since When Have Men Ever Organised Christmas?* Ma Kringle had laughed at that one but, on seeing her husband's grim face, quickly conceded that such gestures of defiance did not help the Kringles out of their plight. Kriss had, therefore, postponed putting forward the motion about inheritance until this year.

The radio crackled into life. "Flight USA Heavy, this is Korvanturi Air Traffic Control, please state your position." "Twelve miles west of approach, Korvanturi. Please advise." Kriss pulled the reins back slightly. It was time to slow down for landing.

"Flight USA Heavy, please take up a holding pattern. There are three sleighs circling the runway at the moment."

Ma Kringle made a noise of disapproval. "I knew we should have had the conference in Canada. One runway is just not enough!"

Kriss sighed. His wife had got her dander up, that was for sure. She was going to make her presence felt this year, come what may.

"Korvanturi, we copy. Assuming holding pattern."
Kriss put the reins on automatic pilot. (Actually he tied the reins to the door handle, making the right hand rein shorter than the left so

that the reindeer would go round in a circle. Technology in the Kringle household was still not up to speed.) He leant back in his seat and looked over at his daughter, asleep in the back, covered in quilts, and he gave a small but worried smile.

Ma Kringle caught the look and patted her husband's hand.

"She's a good girl" she said softly "The best helper you ever had. You know she can do the job."

Kriss nodded. He couldn't have been prouder of his daughter. He knew she would be a fabulous Christmas Gift Bringer. But he also knew that centuries of male tradition was entrenched in the heart of the Yule dynasty and most of the conference would erupt into extremely vocal disapproval.

"There are many who will support you." Ma said, reading her husband's mind.

"Like who?" Kriss muttered wearily.

"Well there are all the existing Female Gift Bringers, for a start. La Befana, Babushka, St Lucy from Switzerland, Tant Arie, the Christmas Lady from Canada and Tante Arie from France… and…and lots of the wives will support the motion."

"They don't count." Kriss said without thinking and then realised what he had said. "I don't mean that they don't count as people…"

"I should hope not," Ma snapped at him.

"I mean the wives, as you know, don't have a vote at the conference, so they don't count."

"But they can still support the idea," she persisted. "I mean what about the host country, Finland? Their Old Man Christmas is in exactly the same position as us. They've only got one daughter."

"Yes, but she's only five years old and his wife is expecting another child any day, which could be a boy."

Kriss sat forward again as the radio crackled into life once more.

"Flight USA Heavy, please turn four degrees north and begin descent. The runway is clear now."

"Roger, Korvanturi, beginning descent now."

Kriss unhitched the reins and began to ease the reindeer around into the course he had been given.

"Besides..." he returned to the topic they had been discussing, "the opposition is going to be enormous. The Europeans might be a little more open-minded, perhaps. I can see Pere Noel of France being persuaded, he's used to a female gift bringer – maybe SinterKlaas of Holland - but can you see Santa Kurohsu of Japan or Dun Che Lao Ren of China being happy about the proposal?"

Kriss now turned his entire attention to the business of landing. The runway lights were coming up fast and it had begun to snow quite heavily, the flakes were driving across his vision and making visibility poor. Consequently, the landing was a little bumpy, waking Christine up from her deep sleep.

"Are we there, Pa?" she said sleepily, her face flushed from the warmth of her quilted nest in the back of the sleigh.

"We're here, honey." Kriss grunted a little as he pulled back on the reins to cut the speed of the eight powerful beasts and stop them taking off again. As they slowed down to a trot, a ground controller appeared, only his eyes were visible through the gap in his Arctic clothing, and he waved his paddles to indicate the direction to be taken.

Kriss wheeled the reindeer expertly and made towards the hangar, which was just a glow of light in the worsening weather. Inside there was warmth and noise and the biggest menagerie of animals ever seen in one building.

The Kringle sleigh eased into position beside a more modest vehicle, pulled by only four reindeer. Kriss instantly recognised Santa of England's sleigh.

"It looks so much smaller than ours" said Ma with a smile, nodding towards it.

"Well, it's only a small country," said Kriss, admiring the craftwork. "These European models, whilst they have half the power of ours, are so beautifully made."

The Kringle family clambered out of their sleigh and stretched their stiff joints. Christine immediately gave each of the reindeer a carrot, speaking to them all softly, then she looked around at the packed hangar.

"Are we the last to arrive, Pa?" she asked.

There certainly didn't seem to be any room for any other vehicles or animals. She counted at least six reindeer teams; then there were the goats which pulled the sleighs of the Swedish and Danish members of the dynasty; horses; donkeys and a large number of camels, belonging to the Kings who brought gifts to the South American countries. Right over in the far corner of the vast hangar were three inanimate modes of travel – a canoe which belonged to Kanakaloka (the Hawaiian Santa); a power boat owned by the Australian Santa (or OzNick to his friends) and a gleaming new Ferrari – red, shiny and extremely powerful. The Kringles all looked at each other. "Babbo Natale," they said in unison, with a knowing smile.

Suddenly, an elf presented himself in front of them, or rather he was a tomte, the Arctic form of elf, wearing a strange and colourful Lapland costume, with the four-pointed headgear which always reminded Christine of a jester's hat.

"Good day Mr and Mrs Kringle and daughter," he said respectfully, "I am Einar and I am your host for the conference. I will show you to your rooms and please feel free to page me whenever you need assistance." Einar handed over a mobile pager and a conference programme. Kriss flicked through it superficially.

"You are scheduled to give your talk on Thursday, Mr Kringle." Einar pointed at page three of the programme. "We are all looking forward to it immensely." Kriss knew that the pleasant tomte was only being polite. When the conference was being put together, the organiser, Black Peter, the right hand man of SinterKlaas of Holland, had said that not that many of the delegates would be interested in Kriss' talk on *Light Pollution and How It Affects Reindeer Radar.*

"Many of them, of course, do not use reindeer," he had said

patronisingly, "but it would be an interesting addition to the programme."

"Please follow me." Einar was leading the way out of the hangar and into the complex. It was a magnificent structure of pine and glass. The foyer, with its vaulted ceiling, was ablaze with Christmas lights and, in the centre, stood the largest Norwegian fir tree that Christine had ever seen, apart from the tree that stood in Times Square in New York every year. Behind the tree were the great entrance doors to the conference hall. The foyer was a fever of arriving delegates and their families.

Christine loved the whole thing. She particularly loved all the different national costumes. Some of the Santa's wore green robes, others wore red. She laughed to see OzNick, who wore a summer shirt and shorts with a traditional fur-trimmed red hat. Surely he must be cold! There was a whole posse of Kings, of course, and the splendour of their costumes was quite something to behold. Leading off the main foyer were carved wooden archways and pine-panelled corridors. Einar had indicated that this was where the guest rooms were located.

"Actually," observed Ma Kringle "this is much better than Canada. Everything's under one roof. I mean, I liked all the individual log cabins in the woods, but it was so cold, traipsing from the cabins to the conference hall. This is much more practical."

They made little progress towards their rooms due to the constant greetings that had to be made to other members of the dynasty that were milling about the foyer and the corridors. There was an air of feverish excitement. The annual conference always took place at the end of November, before everyone's work started. It was the only time that most of them were reunited with each other and there were many loud and emotional expressions of joy. Christine was clasped to many bosoms as various wives remarked how she had grown, how pretty she was and how much they would love a daughter. But she didn't like the way that the wife of Dun Che Lao Ren of China eyed her up. She turned her this way and that, as though she were a horse.

"Good bone structure" she announced to her husband. "Is she healthy?" she asked Ma Kringle.

"Very" said Ma firmly, propelling Christine away. "The cheek of it!" she muttered, when they were out of earshot.

"What was all that about, Ma?" asked a puzzled Christine.

"There is a severe shortage of girls in China, sweetheart." Ma explained. "She's got six sons and she's looking for a wife for each of them."

"Gross!!" Christine shuddered and looked back at the Chinese family and the six boys, aged from two to eighteen, who were staring at her fixedly.

Ma Kringle gritted her teeth but managed a halfway decent smile for the wife of St.Mikulas of Slovakia, who was advancing towards them rapidly.

"Ma Kringle! How have you been my dear?" Mrs St. Mikulas was jolly, kind and very round. She clasped Christine to her bosom and patted her back vigorously. "Such a beautiful girl. You are so lucky. How I would love to have a pretty girl to dress in pretty clothes – instead of my lump of a boy." She inclined her head over and the Kringle family looked at St.Mikulas Junior. He did, indeed look like a lump, Christine thought. A lump with a pudding face and spots. He scowled at them.

"Teenagers!" said his mother with a strong note of irritation in her voice. "Micky, stand up straight and stop sulking!" Micky scowled even more and sloped off. Socialising wasn't his thing at the moment.

Ma Kringle patted Mrs St.Mikulas' arm reassuringly. She would have liked to believe the woman but she knew that they all pitied the Kringles because they did not have a son and it hardened her resolve that, this year, something would be done.

Finally, they reached their rooms – two adjoining bedrooms with bathrooms and one little lounge between.

"Very comfortable, very cosy," Ma Kringle remarked. Pa Kringle tipped Einar generously and ignored his wife's raised eyebrows.

"You never know when you might need an elf to work above and beyond the call of duty," he said when Einar had gone. "It never hurts to buy a little loyalty."

The management had placed complimentary gingerbread and mulled wine on the table and soft carols were playing over the loudspeaker system. The lounge had a log fire crackling away in a grate and Christine sat before it, listening to her mother criticising the rest of the Dynasty, while her father wearily pulled his boots off.

"Did you see the state of that boy of Pere Noel's? It's a disgrace that a boy should be that fat at that age. What are they feeding him on?"

"The Yule's are genetically disposed towards being fat. You know that, woman." Kriss replied, feeling grumpy and tired.

"There's a difference between pleasantly plump and grossly obese. That child won't fit down any chimneys by the time he's fully grown. And did you notice how many times Mrs Belsnickle referred to her son's hockey medal? I don't think it's any big deal to play hockey for Canada. Everyone plays hockey in Canada. I'm sure that lots of boys could qualify for the Canadian hockey team if they wanted to…" Her voice trailed off. She realised that she was being unpleasant because she was upset. She looked at Christine. Her beautiful, wise, kind, fourteen year old daughter, that she wouldn't trade for a whole houseful of boys, and a small tear trickled down her cheek. Kriss Kringle put his arm round his wife's shoulders and planted a kiss on the other cheek.

"Now Ma," he said softly, "we knew it was going to be a difficult job, coming here this year. Don't worry. We're just sleigh-lagged. It's a long trip from the States. A cup of mulled wine, some gingerbread, a bath and a good night's sleep and we'll be our old selves again." He raised his voice and injected as much determination into it as he possibly could. "The Kringles can take on the world!" He gave Ma another vigorous squeeze. Christine looked up from her fire-gazing and smiled.

"Christine is going to be the best Christmas Gift Bringer that the Yule dynasty ever had." Kriss winked at his daughter. "Isn't that right, honey?" Christine nodded and went over to her parents.

"That's right," Ma said through her tears. "Group hug." Christine felt herself enveloped in love and, she reflected, it smelt of reindeer liniment (Pa) and cinnamon (Ma). She looked up at both her parents. "Don't worry, it'll all turn out right."

Kriss gazed over her head into the distance. He smiled and said "Sure it will," but he wasn't sure he believed it.

☆

Chapter two

The Sisterhood

Ma Kringle screamed with delight, *"Beeee!"* and flung her arms open wide to embrace the glamorous elderly Italian woman standing in the doorway of the Kringle suite. La Befana was probably Ma's best friend in the world. Pa Kringle had given up moaning about the size of the phone bill caused by Ma's regular monthly gossips with her soul mate.

"Mama Kringle!" The two women hugged each other strenuously.

Hovering behind La Befana were other members of The Sisterhood, waiting their turn to hug and kiss their friend from America. Christine's face broke into a big smile as she, too, hovered, knowing that it would be her turn next for the barrage of affection.

One by one they came into the room – Babushka, a dour Russian woman, her head swathed in its usual shawl; St.Lucy, of Switzerland, with her long braids and her round cap; the two Tante Arie's, one dressed in Paris chic and the other dressed in furs, like a little French Canadian Inuit; Santa Lucia from Sicily and St.Lucia from Sweden, both with their crowns of four lit candles.

"Hasn't she grown!"

"Look at her lovely chestnut hair!"

"Such beautiful brown eyes!"

The Sisterhood always made Christine feel special. The compliments were sincere and Ma glowed with pride.

"I can't stay long," said Lucy, after cuddling Christine for a while. "I'm supposed to be in charge of the crèche. I've left some tomtes overseeing things for the moment but they are just as naughty as the children."

"Typical." Bee was scornful. "They always give the 'caring' jobs to the women."

"They never give me the crèche job," Paris Arie commented.

Lucy tried to be diplomatic. "Well, dear, that's because you have a reputation for hitting naughty children with your birch switch. I'm sorry dear, but it's true." The glare from Paris Arie made Lucy nervous, Christine could tell.

"That is absolutely as it should be." The Frenchwoman was acidic with righteousness. "If you ask me, not enough naughty children are punished nowadays. All these male Santas do is hand out presents. I haven't seen a child given a piece of coal in his stocking for years."

"Huh!" Babushka was scornful. "Children in the West have too much anyway. Leaving out *sacks and pillowcases* for Santa. It's just plain greedy. In Russia children put out a small pair of shoes. It's quite enough!"

"It's always left to the women to hand out discipline." Bee's unrelenting feminism was just too much for Pa Kringle and he made his excuses.

"Well, ladies,it's been nice to see you again, but I have conference business to discuss, if you'll excuse me." He planted a kiss on the top of Christine's head and propelled his wife out of the door by her elbow.

"Don't let that pack of old biddies talk you into anything controversial" he hissed a warning to Ma in the corridor. "We want to put our proposal forward to the conference without any fuss and bother. Just a reasonable request. No demonstrations, no violent action. Understand?"

"Pa, don't be silly. The girls are just here for a chat. Nothing more."

Kriss looked unconvinced. He remembered the conference in Sweden two years ago when La Befana organised a sit-in on the second day because she didn't like the mini skirts worn by the female elves.

"*Just...*" he tried to emphasise as clearly as he could the importance of the word, "*just* have egg nog and a chat. No hatching schemes or anything. OK?"

"OK. Now off you go and start lobbying." She gave him a reassuring peck on the cheek and watched him walk down the corridor. His shoulders were hunched defensively. She knew he wasn't looking forward to this conference, but what could she do?

"Ma!" La Befana's voice was getting strident, "put that husband of yours down and come back in here – we've business of our own to discuss!" On reflection, Ma thought, maybe Pa's anxieties about The Sisterhood are valid. What were the girls plotting now?

"I'm coming!" she called back cheerily and stepped back into the room once more.

Down in the foyer, the delegates were milling about, making deals and alliances in their usual manner. Every year it was the same, Kriss reflected. Everyone's got an angle – some scheme that they want to get up and running – some deal that they want to make.

Over in the corner, seated in a leather armchair, surrounded by very large and intimidating elves, was Grandfather Frost from Russia. He had not been a happy Santa since the Soviet Union crumbled. Suddenly, a very large chunk of his empire had vanished overnight and minor cousins from the Yule Dynasty had reasserted their rights to be Father Christmas over their own region. Last year, he had tried to move in on Azerbaijan, because the Father Christmas there was making a poor job of it, but the former Soviet regions had banded together to fight off this takeover. Now, they had formed an alliance called TOOFSS (The Order of Former Soviet Santa's) to protect themselves against any future plans hatched by the Russian.

But that wasn't all of the man's troubles. Religion had revived in Russia with a vengeance and Babushka, the Female Gift Bringer, who had the backing of the Orthodox Church, had taken the lead in the polls. The cherry on top of the cake was that the current Babushka was *his mother*. So every time he tried to undermine the popularity of Babushka, she just came round to his house and boxed his ears. Kriss decided not to bother to try and persuade the Russian to vote for his proposal. It would be a lost cause.

He turned his attention to the other corner of the room. Babbo Natale was seated in another armchair, squeezing a stress ball in each hand. He was flanked by some very sharply dressed elves wearing dark glasses. Pathetic! Kriss thought to himself. Who do they think they are? Mafioso? Kriss smirked but then reflected that maybe it wasn't such a joke. There had been a lot of speculation last year about the source of Babbo Natale's toys. Rumours about extortion rackets and exploited elves. Other rumours about unco-operative toy manufacturers suddenly going bankrupt. He shuddered involuntarily. The whole Italian scene made him uncomfortable. La Befana brought him out in hives, she was so militant. Fortunately for Babbo Natale, she was not his mother, but she was a very good friend of the Pope and, therefore, invincible. There was also the problem that Santa Lucia had the sole gift concession in Sicily, a place where Babbo Natale had never been able to get as much as a toe-hold. Nope, that was another Santa not worth approaching.

So, Kriss decided to concentrate on some of the small groups littered around the foyer and he plumped for tackling the Nordic faction first. He wandered up to the first group, consisting of Jultomten of Sweden, Julermanden of Denmark, Old Man Christmas of Finland, and Julenisse of Norway. He would tackle the nine Jole Sveinars of Iceland later, because they could never agree on anything.

"Kriss! Welcome, welcome!" Old Man Christmas was in an expansive mood, as his country was hosting the conference and he had the job of Chairman. "Was the flight good? Are your rooms comfortable?"

Kriss forced a smile on his face and assured his host that everything was just peachy. Ma was "over the moon" with the facilities and the Kringle family couldn't be happier.

"I saw your lovely daughter, when you arrived." Jultomten said kindly but then he added the stinger "Still no son, my friend?"

Kriss took a deep breath. "Actually, I want to put forward a proposal regarding that matter."

The Nordic Santas looked quizzically at him, so he ploughed on.

"I want to propose that Yule Dynasty members be given the right to pass the job on to a daughter."

There. He's said it. It didn't seem so bad, now he'd actually said it. Old Man Christmas looked serious.

"You intend to put forward this proposal after we have read the minutes of the last conference?" he asked.

"Yes."

There was a certain amount of sucking breath in through their teeth, while the group pondered this momentous piece of news.

Julermanden spoke first.

"Personally, I can see your predicament, Kriss, and I sympathise, but such a proposal would create more problems than it would solve."

Kriss was puzzled. "How?"

Julermanden continued. "Well, it would raise the spectre of parental favouritism, for a start. I mean, I love my son dearly, but I have always *trusted* my daughter more. She can always be relied on to do her homework, tidy her room, behave well and so on. If I were suddenly able to make a decision about my business based on an objective evaluation of my children, I might consider handing it over to my daughter instead of my son, and that would create bad feeling."

Julenisse intervened.

"But wait a minute, there. Kriss is not necessarily proposing that we give the option, is he? Are you?" he asked Kriss, who was now so flummoxed that he didn't really know what to say.

"I…I..don't think so."

Julenisse looked triumphant, as though he, and only he, had the intelligence to understand Kriss' proposal.

Julenisse continued, "What Kriss is suggesting is that the ability to hand on the job to the female offspring should only be exercised when there *is no option*. Isn't that right?"

There was a general murmuring of "Aahs" and "I see's". Kriss waited until someone put the whole thing into plain English.

Old Man Christmas took up the baton. "Then any proposal would have to be very carefully worded so that there was no room for abuse. It would have to state clearly that the passing down of the business to a daughter could only take place if there were no son in the family."

Kriss began to feel a flutter of hope. "So are you saying that you guys would approve such a proposal…if it were worded correctly?" he asked hesitantly.

Jultomten nodded sagely. "Speaking personally, I think I could probably be persuaded that, in extenuating circumstances such as yours, there would be a case for passing through the female line."

Kriss took that for a yes and turned excitedly to Old Man Christmas.

"Would it be possible for you and I to meet up later and draft the proposal?"

"Absolutely!" the Finn slapped Kriss on the back heartily. "I shall be only too pleased to help. Come and see me after lunch in meeting room four and we shall thrash it out."

"Thank you, thank you." Kriss pumped hands in gratitude and, spirits soaring, moved on to tackle a much harder proposition – the South American group. Could he think of the right words to appeal to their macho sensibilities? Never mind. He would give it a go.

Back in the Kringle suite, Christine had lost interest in the conversation around her. After the initial warmth and pleasantries, La Befana had degenerated into her usual rant against men folk in general. Sure, she was funny. The joke about the English Santa who got lost over the North Sea because he wouldn't stop and ask directions, was good. What *is it* about men and asking directions? Christine mused. But, mostly, the Italian woman came across as bitter and envious.

Christine reflected on Pa's favourite saying. "A little sweetness goes a long way. You catch more flies with honey than with vinegar." He meant, of course, that people responded better to kindness than to criticism. So when St.Lucy announced that she really had to get back to the crèche, Christine leapt at the chance to leave and asked if she could go with her. Ma beamed and agreed it was a good idea. So Lucy and Christine left the other women to their egg nog and gossip.

Christine liked Lucy. She actually worked in partnership with Samichlaus of Switzerland – well she had to - she was married to him. She gave presents to the girls and her husband gave presents to the boys. Trust the Swiss to work out an efficient system. But Lucy was naturally very kind. She saw everyone's point of view and wanted to help everybody. She knew that the Kringles were in a difficult position and while membership of The Sisterhood did not sit easily on her shoulders, she wanted to support Christine's bid to become America's Female Gift Bringer.

"After all, I'm sure you'll have a female President one day. Why not a female Santa? If anyone can do it, the Americans can." Lucy was nothing if not reasonable. If only, thought Christine, the rest of the Yule Dynasty was reasonable too.

The creche was, as St.Lucy had feared, in total chaos.

"Oh my lord!" she wailed, as they stepped through the door. It looked like an explosion in a Christmas decoration factory. There was glitter glue smeared on the walls, glitter dust all over the floor, the eighteen Icelandic boys were having a bauble fight and the two Russian boys had tied up the Slovakian boy with tinsel. The three tomtes supposedly in charge were shouting, to no avail, and the noise level was unbearable.

"STOP IT AT ONCE OR I SHALL FETCH THE BLACK GANG!" Lucy's very, very loud threat produced instant silence. One small Dutch boy began to whimper and various lips started trembling.

It's astonishing the effect that the Black Gang have on kids, Christine marvelled. The Black Gang, of course, were all the nasty helpers of various European Santas. They dressed in black and it was their job to beat all the naughty children while Santa rewarded all the good children. Black Peter of Holland was their leader, then there was Knecht Ruprecht of Northern Germany, Krampus of Southern Germany, Hans Muff from the Rhineland, Cert from the Czech Republic, Schmutzli from Switzerland and several others.

Thankfully, the Kringle family did not have such a helper in the USA but Christine shared the same dread of The Black Gang as all the other children. At the annual conferences she had seen them roaming the corridors, sticks in hand, looking for unruly children to beat. Babbo Natale's two sons currently held the record for the most thwacks on the backside from a member of the Black Gang but then they were always up to some sort of devilment and, in Christine's opinion, probably deserved it. Not that it seemed to make any impression on them. They just carried on, every year, causing trouble. Last year, at the Canadian conference, they had inserted firecrackers into the giant Christmas tree so, when the candles were lit for the closing ceremony, the whole tree exploded like a hail of machine gun bullets.

Order having been restored in the crèche, Lucy cleaned off the distressed tomtes while Christine made all the children a drink.

"I have to say," Lucy said quietly to Christine "that the Yule Dynasty sets a bad example to the rest of the world. There we all are, judging everyone else's children at Christmas time and we don't pay enough attention to disciplining our own offspring. In fact, I've a good mind to raise the matter at the conference tomorrow."

Christine sighed. Anyone who thought that Santa was a jolly old soul, whose life was one long round of candy canes and

Christmas songs, should come to one of these conferences. It would certainly be an eye-opener.

"Why don't you go along to the teenage pop-in parlour?" Lucy suggested helpfully. Inwardly, Christine groaned. The dreaded teenage pop-in parlour was a kind-of games room that the organisers of these conferences set up every year. Last year, there had only been two girls there, apart from herself. The thought of socialising with a lot of teenage boys did not fill her with joy. However, there seemed to be no option. The crèche held minimal appeal and the thought of going back to her room and listening to The Sisterhood moaning about the Yule men was even less appealing.

She would just have to give it a try. After all, if Pa succeeded in getting the delegates to agree on female succession to "the job", the boys would, eventually, be her colleagues. "You just have to work a bit harder when the sleigh is heavier," as Pa would say. So, with a deep breath, she set off to beard the young lions in their den, so to speak.

☆

CHAPTER THREE

Shared Secrets

Christine wandered along the corridor to the teenage pop-in parlour. It was three doors away from the crèche. Lucy had told her that it was provided with a viewing gallery so that the teenagers could observe the conference, when it started.

She pushed open the door and her heart sank as she surveyed the room. Babbo Natale's two boys were playing pool; the very large son of Pere Noel of France was sitting in the corner eating a bag of doughnuts; while, in one corner, two boys were playing chess. She decided the chess players were her best bet so she strolled casually over to them, ignoring the wolf whistles from the Italians.

"Hi, I'm Christine Kringle" she said hopefully, only to be rewarded by a scowl from one boy, while the other boy leapt up, bowed and said "Pleased to meet you. I have the honour to be Little K, son of Santa Kurohsu of Japan."

Christine smiled and shook his hand. Then she turned to the other boy. "And you are?"

The tall, thin boy with blonde hair held out a hand, without really looking at her. "Young Nick, from England," he mumbled.

"Oh cool! I've always wanted to meet a member of the English family… and the Japanese family, of course," she added hastily, ever the diplomat. "Can I sit with you?" She pulled up a chair without waiting for a reply.

"Please yourself," was the diffident reply from Nick.

"We would be honoured," was the enthusiastic reply from

Little K.

There was a moment's silence whilst Nick toyed uncomfortably with a chess piece. Christine decided he needed drawing out.

"I've never seen either of you at the conference before. Is this your first visit?" she asked cheerily.

"Boarding school," was the non-commital reply from Nick.

"Military school," was the pleasant reply from Little K.

Christine's response to this was drowned out by a sudden eruption of fighting between the two Italians and the French boy. One of the Natale's had tried to take Pere Noel Junior's last doughnut. The normally slothful heavyweight had been roused by this hideous crime and was laying into the Italians with his fists – having made sure that the doughnut in question was safely stuffed into his mouth first. Thus, the fight took place in a hail of spat-out dough and jam. The Italians beat a hasty, and sticky, retreat, realising that they had made a bad move and that doughnut-boy was pretty lethal when his food supply was threatened.

Christine made a face of disgust as the French boy beamed at them, soggy doughnut squeezing through his teeth and jam trickling down his chin. Then he left, presumably to get more food.

"Good grief, just look at the rubbish he's left behind him!" she said, pointing to the sugar-encrusted bag on the floor and the sweet wrappers littering the chair. As she moved to clear it up, the door opened and there stood Black Peter. The room suddenly got twenty degrees colder.

His black eyes glittered in his thin sallow face as he surveyed the litter. "Is this your debris?" he hissed menacingly.

"N...no, sir," Christine found herself stuttering. Why was it that members of the Black Gang could inspire such fear in any child they approached?

"Then it must have been one of you." The black-clad inquisitor turned his attention to Nick and Little K.

Little K shook his head vigorously. Black Peter lifted one of his arched eyebrows even higher and fixed his gaze on Nick. The sullen teenager stared back at him defiantly. "Not me, man." The reply was insolent and Black Peter made a sharp intake of breath through his nostrils.

He scuttled across the room, his thin black-stockinged legs making him look like a malevolent spider and he bent low, bringing his face very close to Nick's. He smiled maliciously. "Having an overload of testosterone that, mistakenly, makes you feel like you are a man?"

Nick flinched but said nothing. Black Peter continued. "Well, you are not a man – yet. You are still a child and, under Rule 17 Section 8 Paragraph 4 of the Yule Dynasty Charter, I am still allowed to hit you with my birch switch and I can do so until you reach the age of 16. Understand?"

Nick, looking rather pale, simply nodded and his tormentor unbent himself and looked satisfied. "Who made this mess?" He looked at Christine again but no-one said anything.

Black Peter pursed his lips in annoyance. "Very well. As you have this misguided notion that you do not tell tales about each other, you will have to clear it up on behalf of the real criminal. You will all come to my office now and collect cleaning implements." He scuttled over to the door and opened it wide. "At once...now...move."

The three teenagers silently filed out of the doorway and followed Black Peter down the corridor. Most children shot them pitying glances as they passed, assuming that Black Peter was taking them for punishment. Christine was simmering quietly with rage. She decided she was going to make the French and Italian boys pay for this indignity. The only question was, how?

Outside Black Peter's office there was a gaggle of the Black Gang, awaiting orders. They all sniggered as their leader swept into his room, followed by the teenagers. "Knecht Ruprecht!" he bawled through the open door and the called-for-one appeared. "Fetch a rubbish sack, a dustpan and brush and some disinfectant spray." Ruprecht hurried off to the store rooms. Black Peter sat in his desk and surveyed the massive chart on the wall in front of him.

"Do you see that chart?" he snapped at them. The three miscreants nodded. "That chart," Black Peter continued "represents ten months of intensive work. It shows every delegate's times of arrival and departure, accommodation needs, conference programme, food requirements and more. The annual Yule Conference is a logistical nightmare. And it is my logistical nightmare. I flatter myself that I do a good job. Every little detail is covered except...except for the behaviour of loathsome children, like you."

Christine opened her mouth to protest but thought better of it when a gleam appeared in Black Peter's eye. She knew he would like nothing better than to give her a good thwack with his birch switch. It might damage Pa Kringle's chances of getting the inheritance proposal passed if her name went into the punishment book.

"Yes?" Black Peter was almost eager for her to say something.

"I just wanted to say sorry and that it will never happen again." Christine ignored the angry glare from Nick.

Black Peter seemed almost disappointed but he acknowledged the apology with a grunt. Knecht Ruprecht appeared with the cleaning materials and the three of them were sent back to the pop-in parlour to do their task.

"How could you apologise to him like that for something that we didn't do?" Nick said accusingly, when they were outside the office.

"It was the simplest way. Trust me." Christine was not going to explain about the Kringle family mission in a crowded corridor.

"No, she was right to apologise." Little K insisted. "In my country, you accept responsibility for everything. We should have stopped the fight and we should have made them clean up."

"IT'S NOT TOO LATE!!" Nick's voice rose to a shout as he spotted the French boy turning the corner. He bounded after him, grabbed him in an arm lock and propelled him towards the litter-strewn room. "You clean up your own mess, mon ami, or I'm going to force feed you that rubbish sack!"

"OK, OK." The French boy decided to capitulate and the three of them stood over him as he picked up all the debris. Christine felt sorry for him and bent down to wield the dustpan and brush because his size made it difficult for him to bend over. The other two just sat down and watched silently.

"OK, c'est fini, yes?" Pere Noel Junior mumbled hopefully. He was basically a genial soul, despite being greedy and lazy, and Christine said "Yes" and gave him a smile. He ambled off gratefully.

"You were too soft." said Nick scornfully.

Christine just smiled and presented Nick with the bag of rubbish and the cleaning implements. "Now be a good English boy and take all this stuff back to Black Peter's office. Then you can both come back to my place and have some hot chocolate."

Nick snorted but Christine sensed that he thought she was an OK person really. "We'll meet you by the tree in the main hall!" she called after him as he disappeared down the corridor.

"Yeah, whatever," he called back over his shoulder.

Christine, Little K, Young Nick and Pere Noel Junior

Christine and Little K stood in silence by the giant tree in the hallway, marvelling at all the fabulous ornaments. They were not alone. Every passer-by seemed to stop for at least five minutes to stare in wonder at its beauty. The tree was covered with tiny toys; gold and silver baubles; red and white candy canes; shimmering lights; red bows; tiny wooden reindeer; shiny gilded apples and nuts; – oh, so many things. You could stand in front of it every day and still spot something you hadn't seen before. However, thanks to the Natale boys' prank of last year, the tree was surrounded by a six foot high Perspex barrier, which prevented anyone from getting close. It's a shame, Christine reflected, that the actions of a few always penalise everyone else.

Nick joined them and they made their way to the Kringle's suite. The Sisterhood had left, and Ma was just about to go shopping at the Craft Market on the other side of the conference complex. She beamed to see Christine with the two boys.

"How lovely that you have some new friends already! Come in, come in." She ushered them into the warm room. "I'll make you some hot chocolate before I go out."

"No, Ma," Christine protested gently "I can do it. Don't fuss. We're just going to hang out here for a while. You go shopping. Go on."

"Well, if you're sure. It was nice to meet you boys," she smiled warmly at them as she left and they both smiled politely back, which reassured her that they were nice boys and suitable friends.

"Hot chocolate and gingerbread?" Christine headed for the hospitality tray in her parent's room.

"Yes please" said Little K.

"I don't want any gingerbread thanks – the stuff makes me sick," Nick said hastily.

The others looked at him in astonishment. Yules ate gingerbread all the time. Baby Yules cut their teeth on hard gingerbread and elderly Yules munched on soft gingerbread. It was part of their staple diet.

"I've never heard of that before." Christine was curious.

"Yeah, well, I'm not your average Yule, I guess." Nick sounded a little defensive. "Ever since I got to the age of twelve, I can't stand gingerbread and the smell of cinnamon gives me a migraine. In fact I can't stand Christmas at all OK?"

Christine looked at him with concern. "What other problems do you have, Nick? It sounds like the food thing is just the tip of the iceberg."

Nick looked depressed. "My mother is not a Yule, right? I mean, she isn't a regular human or anything, she's…a tall elf."

"Wow!" Christine couldn't think of anything else to say.

"I have seen a tall elf!" Little K was quite excited. "When we went to Sweden on holiday, we saw a really tall elf. Taller than me. Very interesting." Little K was a bit of a boffin and *everything* interested him. "It also means that you will live longer. Yes?"

"Yeah." Nick didn't seem too overjoyed at the prospect. "Male elves live, on average, for 902 years, but the downside is that puberty lasts for an average of twenty seven years."

There was a silence while his two new friends entered into a communal feeling of horror at that particular fate.

So, like, I have certain problems." Nick decided he could trust them.

"Like what?" Christine was sympathetic.

"Like The Transmogrification."

Christine's hand flew to her mouth. The Transmogrification was the single most important feat that a Yule Gift Bringer had to be able to accomplish. The ability to transmogrify from human form to magic dust atoms and back again into human form, for the passage down through a chimney, was genetically programmed into every Yule. Teenagers started practising around their twelfth birthday and, by the age of fourteen or fifteen, were usually completely skilled. Christine had never had any problems. In fact, by the time she was thirteen she could transmogrify so quickly that it had hardened her father's resolve to ask for the inheritance law to be changed. She felt a wave of pity for Nick.

"Can you do it at all?" she enquired tentatively.

Nick looked uncomfortable. "It's patchy. I never know if it's going to work or not."

"Perhaps you are a late developer" said Little K helpfully. "My cousin was not able to do it until he was seventeen."

Nick looked relieved. "Really? Seventeen? Cool..."

Christine nodded. "Yes I'm sure that's what it is. I've known girls who have never developed the skill at all. Mind you, they probably never tried, so they probably could have done, if they'd wanted to."

"Listen," Nick sounded a little desperate "I don't know why I told you guys, but please don't tell anyone else."

"No way! Cross my heart and hope to die." Christine said firmly.

"I would never betray a confidence." Little K was very earnest.

"Thanks man." Nick nodded gratefully.

"Anyway, I have a secret too." Christine felt like confiding. "Let me get the hot chocolate and then I'll tell you."

As they slowly sipped their hot drinks, Christine told them all about the Kringle family mission to change the inheritance law of the Yule Dynasty at this year's conference. Nick was impressed.

"Awesome. I don't see why girls shouldn't do the job. In fact you're lucky. I'd give anything not to become the English Santa Claus. I hate the whole Christmas thing. I hate being called Nick Christmas for a start. You have no idea how much grief that has caused me at boarding school. You'd think my father could have been more creative."

Christine sympathised. She, too, had had a spell at a boarding school where she had taken the name of Christine Holiday. It hadn't worked out, because of extreme homesickness, so now she went to elf school in the Kringle compound up in the Colorado mountains.

Little K tried to be supportive about the female gift bringer option but he was too scientific by nature and he started to debate as to whether females had enough muscle power to drive a big sleigh and whether children would accept a female Santa Claus. His two new friends just looked at him, so he decided to drop the matter and tell them his own secret instead.

From his trouser pocket he withdrew a small bundle – something wrapped in a cloth. He stood in front of a floor lamp and opened the cloth and, immediately, about one metre of highly flexible cord, with inbuilt Christmas lights and no visible power supply, leapt from his hand and wound itself around the lamp. Christine and Nick stood in open-mouthed astonishment. Little K then peeled the cord from the lamp, as though it were a living creature, like a snake, and threw it upwards towards a large picture that was hanging over the fireplace. The lights automatically draped themselves in a swag over the top of the picture frame. Christine laughed.

"Can I have a go?" she asked eagerly.

Little K nodded and peeled the lights off the picture frame. They felt warm in Christine's hands and they moved a little, just as though they were alive. Not as bold as her Japanese friend, she decided to *take* them to a door frame, rather than throw them. The lights wriggled around the doorway and elected to drape themselves flat across the top of the frame and hang down, with perfect symmetry, either side.

"They're amazing!" Nick took the lights down and, soon, each of them was taking turns and throwing the lights around the room with abandon.

"I invented them" said Little K, when they all subsided, panting from their energetic game. "I thought they would be great for outdoors and for places without power supplies. No more transformers or batteries."

"What's the power source then?" Nick was keen to know.

Little K looked conspiratorial. "Flying reindeer DNA." Nick whistled softly and Little K continued. "I discovered that one gram of droppings in a melted snow solution will power ten metres of cable."

Christine's lip curled, half in distaste and half in amusement. "You mean this thing runs on reindeer poo?!!"

"Absolutely. Endless source of energy."

"I think they're fabulous and that you are very clever." Christine patted him on the back.

Little K bowed. "Thank you. My father is going to introduce them at tomorrow's conference."

"They should be an instant success." Nick was still playing gently with the lights , which had now wrapped themselves around his legs. "Hey! Look! People could wear them too!"

Little K, however, had some reservations about people wearing the lights.

"When you have a single strand of lights, like this, you can do anything with it. But when there are more than one, in the same room, the reindeer DNA makes the lights act as though they were part of a herd. They all want to be together. It's a small problem. I am confident that I will find the solution."

Christine wrapped the lights around her head and looked in the mirror. She was still young enough to, occasionally, appreciate looking like a fairy princess. Her crown of lights twinkled back at her from the mirror. This, she thought, was going to be the best conference she had ever attended – ever, in her whole life.

☆

CHAPTER FOUR

The Conference Starts

Day one of the conference was filled with anticipation, despite the large number of headaches prevailing amongst the delegates, due to the First Night Banquet.

Christine always adored the Banquet. The food was usually terrific, everyone drank far too much mulled wine and everyone's, but everyone's, parents made complete fools of themselves.

Pa Kringle had ended up on the Christmas Karaoke machine a little earlier than last year. It wasn't that his voice was bad – in fact he had a rather fine baritone – but he had just never grasped the concept of microphones. Consequently, everyone had been blasted out of their seats by his lusty rendition of *Good King Wenceslas* and he had ended up all flushed and sweaty.

St Nicholas of the Czech Republic, in an attempt to embrace Pa Kringle for singing about a Czech folk hero, had tripped over his robe and fallen, face first, into the punchbowl. This had provoked the nine Jole Svienars from Iceland to burst into a furious song (something about a troll falling into a lake) and throw bread roll pellets at the collective Kings from South America, who *always* sat together. Christine felt that there was something so undignified about Kings with bits of bread stuck to their crowns.

Samichlaus from Switzerland had calmed everything down and the Karaoke had resumed with a particularly tuneless rendition, in Japanese, by Santa Kurohsu, of *Hark the Herald Angels Sing*. Some dignity had been finally restored by Bishop Nicholas of the Ukraine and St.Mikulas of Slovakia who had performed a duet of a Russian carol. They sang, tenor and baritone, with such incomparable sweetness, that the room had fallen silent and Ma Kringle had allowed a few tears to trickle down her cheeks.

When the Kringle family had finally tumbled through the door of their suite, it had been past three o'clock in the morning.

In the morning, Pa's fine voice had been a little croaky when he, eventually, surfaced at breakfast. Ma was not sympathetic.

"So what's the order of business today, Pa?" Christine was all eagerness.

Pa took a big swig of coffee and retrieved a crumpled agenda from his pocket.

"First there's the usual opening address from the Chairman, then there are the minutes from last year's conference, then there are three motions on the agenda for today. Number one is from Santa Kurohsu, number two is from Belsnickle of Canada and number three is us."

"What are the other two motions about?" Ma was intrigued.

"I know what Santa Kurohsu's one is!" Christine volunteered and proceeded to tell her parents about the amazing lights that Little K had invented. Ma and Pa Kringle were duly impressed.

"Well that should take the Christmas spirit to some out of the way places." Ma was always positive about everything.

Pa, on the other hand, could always see the drawbacks. "I reckon there might be some opposition to that one," he said gravely. "I can see some of the battery and electrical manufacturers might take it badly. I don't know."

Christine was disappointed. "You should see the lights, Pa. They're so wonderful. It would be a shame if they weren't approved."

Pa Kringle shook his head. "I'm sorry honey. I'm sure they are wonderful but I can just see some opposition to it, that's all."

"What's the Canadian motion going to be about?" Ma asked.

Pa shrugged and made a face. "Oh it's just the usual one that is brought forward every year. The one about making the gift-giving day the same date for everyone."

"Oh not that old chestnut!" Ma snorted.

"Yep. Old Belsnickle drew the short straw this year. The same group of guys keep trying to put this idea forward and it never gets past first base."

Christine knew what they were talking about. Some of the gift givers gave their presents on St Nicholas's Day, which was December 6th – others gave their gifts on Christmas Eve and yet more gave their gifts during Epiphany – some days after Christmas. Every year someone put forward the motion that gift-giving should be standardised to Christmas Eve and, every year, the motion was turned down by all those Gift Bringers who wanted to keep their national traditions.

"What about our motion, Pa? Will it be successful?" she asked anxiously.

Pa Kringle smiled. "Do you know, I think it might be. I spent all day yesterday lobbying the delegates and a surprising number of them said that they would give their support. The Chairman has helped me draft the motion so that the proposal is that inheritance through the female line can only take place if there is no alternative. That means that no-one could choose their daughter instead of their son, if they have one. It should work. I think it might stand a chance."

Ma beamed and ordered a family hug. The Kringle family were ready to face the world. Hopes were high and Pa, after downing another cup of coffee, was ready to take on the conference.

Christine had arranged to meet Nick and Little K in the teenage viewing gallery. They sat there, waiting for the empty conference hall to fill up, and emptied out the contents of their conference "goody bags". Every delegate received one when they arrived, filled with complimentary gifts from the host country. Christine read out the brochure, which explained the contents and the national traditions of Finland. "There are some Joulutortut – those are Finnish Christmas pastries filled with prune jam," she explained helpfully to the others.

Nick pulled a face.

Christine continued "Piparkut – those are ginger cookies..."

Nick pulled an even stronger face of disapproval.

"...and Mustikkpiirakka – blueberry pie..."

Nick looked mildly interested.

"...and Pulla, which is coffee bread ring."

Nick looked approving.

Christine delved deeper into her goody bag, which was actually a Hessian sack decorated with little embroidered tomtes. "Yuk!" she exclaimed, drawing out some garlic sausage, nicely tied into a hoop shape.

"Merveilleux!" the French boy enthused. He had eased his bulk into the seat behind the three friends. Christine promptly handed him the garlic sausage with a relieved smile and he began to untie it and eat.

"Oh this is cute!" she said, pulling out a rather nice wooden advent calendar with little shutters that opened to reveal Christmas pictures.

"It's called a Joulukalenteri," said Little K, scanning his own brochure.

Christine then withdrew a straw angel mobile, a Christmas candle and a pretty lace cap. "It says here that the cap is called a tykkimyssy. It's for girls to wear. What have the boys got?"

Nick and Little K scrabbled around in their sacks and each found a knitted hat and an embroidered belt. "Cool!" said Nick, turning the belt over and over in his hands. "Most acceptable," said Little K, pulling the knitted hat down over his ears and making them all laugh.

"Not a bad haul really," commented Christine, the conference goody bag veteran of the group.

"Yeah, except for the prune jam." Nick handed his pastries over to the French boy, who nodded gratefully and gave Nick his embroidered belt in return. It wouldn't have fitted round his waist anyway.

"Oh I don't know," Christine was happily munching away. "The prune jam is actually rather nice. At last year's conference in Canada, all the pastries and doughnuts were heavy on the maple syrup. Too sweet for me."

There was a small silence while everyone ate something. More garlic sausage was handed back to the French boy, which Christine felt might be a mistake, since the odour emanating from behind them was getting quite strong.

"So what happens this morning?" Nick asked, never having been to a Yule conference before.

"Well…" Christine felt a little tingle of excitement. "The delegates all come in and take their seats…then the Chairman comes in and they all sing the opening song, which is usually the favourite Christmas song of the host country. Pa's been practising it all week," she added by way of information.

"My father too…" Little K sounded less enthusiastic than Christine at the prospect. The others shot him a sympathetic look, remembering Santa Kurohsu's tuneless warbling from the night before.

"Then, it's like a normal business meeting," she continued. "There are apologies for absence; minutes of the last meeting; matters arising from the minutes of the last meeting and then the proposals of the day."

"Sounds boring," said Nick .

"Oh no!" Christine laughed. "I guess if you've never been to a family conference, you wouldn't know…and you being English and reserved and all that…"

"What?" Nick was puzzled.

Christine explained to him some of the events that had taken place during Yule conferences, as far back as she could remember, which was from about when she was eight. "Well, there was the year that La Befana organised a sit-in protest, then there was the conference in Hawaii where Belsnickle of Canada got badly sunburnt and couldn't sit down…"

"Couldn't sit down?"

"Don't ask. He had to do the whole conference standing up and OzNick thought it was so hilarious that he kept smacking him on the bottom every time he passed by. I think that was also the year when there was a protest over pay and conditions by the elves in South American countries. Certain delegates got pelted with wet coffee grounds. Very messy. I know that the conference we hosted in the USA was a riot because Pa had chosen a venue near Lake Tahoe, you know, the place with all the casinos. Several of the delegates couldn't be prised away from the slot machines. In the end they had to send a crack team of elves in to kidnap the gambling addicts and confine them to the conference headquarters."

"So it's not exactly uneventful then?" Nick said sardonically.

"No, it certainly isn't." Christine settled back into her seat in pleasant anticipation. No-one could ever call the Yule Dynasty boring, that was for sure.

Little K nudged Nick. "Something is happening."

A sudden flurry of black-suited beings spread across the chamber like a slick of oil. The Black Gang had arrived and they were busy putting agendas, notepads and pens out. The chamber was tiered, like an amphitheatre and the delegates would sit on cushioned banks with a continuous pine writing surface in front of them. Christine imagined that the United Nations looked similar, with all the country names and the microphones.

The Black Gang disappeared, as silently as they had come, and the delegates began to take their places. Everyone was dressed in their best gift-bringer outfits and, as they milled in, murmuring quietly to each other, Christine marvelled at the rich sea of red, green, gold and white that presented itself. Even OzNick, who usually wore a kind-of beach bum outfit, with a Santa hat, had managed to find a surfing shirt that had Christmas trees all over it – and he was wearing white trousers, rather than his usual ripped-jean shorts.

The various Kings, from the South America countries, looked magnificent, as usual, the gold of their crowns and the rich brocade and jewels of their garments, glowed and sparkled by the light of the main chandelier.

Christine always felt that the female Gift Bringers looked particularly fetching because their costumes reflected their national traditions and heritage. Babushka had exchanged her plain shawl for one embroidered in vivid reds and yellows and her long skirt was a deep red. La Befana wore a red shawl, a white blouse and a green skirt (the colours of the Italian flag) and she carried her badge of office, the broom, in keeping with the legend that Befana preferred to sweep her house rather than accompany the Wise Men to Bethlehem. Christine had seen that broom used to great effect at various conferences, particularly when Babbo Natale upset her. St Lucia from Switzerland and Santa Lucia were wearing battery-operated candle crowns as, last year, the beard of the delegate seated behind them had been singed by their real candles when he nodded off and his head slumped forward.

The delegates took their seats and then all rose again, to honour the entrance of the chairman, Old Man Christmas of Finland, who swept regally down the aisle with his tomte secretaries and took up his position on the podium.

"Welcome, welcome, to the nine hundredth and twenty seventh annual Yule conference. Please remain standing whilst we sing the opening song."

A tomte orchestra, seated in a gallery, high up on the left, began to play a lilting introduction and the magnificent massed voices of the brethren and sisters of the Yule Dynasty, surged into life.

The conference had begun.

☆

CHAPTER FIVE

A Shock Announcement

The first part of the business of the conference passed relatively quickly. There were no apologies for absence and the minutes of the last meeting were passed. Matters arising from the minutes of the last meeting were brief. There was a vote of thanks to the Microsoft Foundation for financing the retraining scheme for elves. Such had been the demand, in recent years, for electronic toys, computer hardware and software, that the traditional elf-skills of carpentry and joinery were beginning to be redundant. It had been decided at last year's conference, to undertake a mass retraining in computer skills. Carpenters and other artisans were still needed, of course, but not in the numbers employed previously.

Few people, outside of the Yule Dynasty, realised that, since the advent of television, in the 1950s, which had created a worldwide surge in the demand for consumer goods, most Christmas toys were, in fact, not made by elves, but manufactured by toy companies under licence. The elves were primarily responsible now for research and development and quality control. In other words, they often invented the toys that were manufactured and they made sure that they were manufactured to the stringent requirements of the Yule Dynasty Manufacturing Handbook.

This change in the working practices of elves had caused considerable difficulties. There had been the Great Elf Strike of 1964 and the Mass Walkout of 1971 but, come the Millennium, most of the elf community had settled down quite happily to their new role in the Christmas manufacturing set-up, especially as they were now considerably better paid.

Of course, these changes had been the fault of the Yule Dynasty itself. Ever at the forefront of smart business practice, the Dynasty had decided to get itself out of a slump in the nineteenth century by a concerted PR campaign. The general public never knew, but the Dynasty had employed several popular writers of the time to give Christmas a boost. Charles Dickens in England was one. His story *A Christmas Carol* revolutionised the public perception of Christmas. Then there was Beatrix Potter, who wrote *The Tailor of Gloucester*. But by far the most significant contribution to the PR campaign had been made by Clement Clarke Moore in America, whose poem *The Night Before Christmas* was single-handedly responsible for the explosion in children's belief in St.Nick. That genius stroke of nineteenth century marketing was still talked of by the current Yule Dynasty as The Great Promotion.

Old Man Christmas announced the first proposal on the agenda. The three teenagers sat forward expectantly. Santa Kurohsu stood and cleared his throat.

"My son..." he waved his hand towards the viewing gallery. Everyone turned to look at Little K, who blushed furiously. Christine and Nick beamed at him encouragingly. "My son," Santa K repeated "has invented some extraordinary Christmas lights, which, we feel, will take the Christmas spirit to new and, hitherto, unreachable places. We feel that they would be as significant a contribution to Christmas as The Great Promotion."

There was a great murmur of astonishment and Santa K nodded, as if to emphasise his claims. "Please bring them in," he called to some unseen elves.

The curtains, at the side of the stage, parted and two elves pushed on a large wheeled basket, covered with a cloth. The cloth, much to the delegate's consternation, was moving. Christine and her friends knew that it was the strings of lights that were writhing around, anxious to be set free to decorate. The delegates murmured uncertainly.

"Please release them," Santa K commanded and the elves whipped off the cloth and began throwing handfuls of what appeared to be twinkling snakes into the air. There were some shocked shouts from delegates and a few shrieks from the Female Gift Bringers, but then the assembly watched in fascinated silence as the lights targeted the chandelier and the galleries, draping themselves into perfect swags, or twining themselves around pillars.

Even Pere Noel Junior stopped eating as several swags hit the glass of the viewing chamber with a thwack, which made the teenagers sit back in their seats. The lights then proceeded to drape themselves into swags along the top of the window.

When all the lights had been thrown out from the basket and had arranged themselves into artistic forms, the shocked assembly, after a moment's silence, burst into applause and cheers.

Santa K looked relieved and Little K was happy to be slapped heartily on the back by Nick and Pere Noel Junior.

However, when the fuss had died down, Christine noticed that the South American contingent were far from happy. "Look!" she pointed and started to giggle.

Six groups of Three Kings stood up together. They had to, really, because the lights had been attracted to the King's crowns and had draped themselves between each crown as a swag, so the Kings were inextricably bound together by festive, twinkling ropes.

"These lights would seem to have a few flaws in their programming," commented a King from Argentina, acidly.

"Yes, I agree," said La Befana loudly, brandishing her broom, which was now a spiral of coloured lights.

There were some strange muffled sounds from the side of the auditorium and two elves rushed to investigate. They discovered that the lights, for some bizarre reason, had flocked to decorate the person of Black Peter. He had been standing so still, observing the conference, that the lights had obviously mistaken him for an inanimate statue. The result was that he now looked like a fairy at the top of a Christmas tree, and, to make matters worse, one of the ropes of lights had bound itself around his mouth. Nick and Christine started laughing but stopped when they realised that Little K was mortified with shame.

Babbo Natale stood up. "Aside from the unpredictability of these lights, there is also the question of the power source. Might I ask the delegate from Japan what it is?"

There was a slight tremble in Santa K's voice when he said "Flying reindeer droppings."

There was a collective intake of breath from the assembled delegates and Babbo Natale's mouth set in a grim line.

"Chairman and delegates. I think I probably speak for all of you when I say that this invention would irretrievably damage our international relationships with electrical manufacturers."

Christine's heart sunk. It was exactly as Pa Kringle had predicted. The Yule Dynasty was not ready for Little K's invention.

The assembly burst into a furious debate. There were many delegates who had been charmed by the lights. Oz Nick was shouting "You're a dinosaur!" at Grandfather Frost from Russia, while Dun Che Lao Ren was trying to make a statement about the manufacturing possibilities of the product in Chinese factories. The Chairman was unable to make himself heard as the arguments became louder and louder.

"I see what you mean about Yule conferences!" shouted Nick in Christine's ear.

Christine leant across to Little K, who was staring fixedly at the floor. "Don't feel badly!" she shouted, rubbing his knee. "They'll come round." Little K looked at her sadly and shook his head.

Suddenly, there was the shrill blast of a whistle. Black Peter, having been released from his bonds, was taking command, in his role as Head of Security. A small silver whistle was between his lips. The first blast had stopped the shouting and the second blast made all the delegates sit down again.

"Thank you, Peter," said the harassed Chairman. "Now…" he

spoke reprovingly and glared at the assembly. "If we can all calm down please. The elves will retrieve the lights and we can proceed with business."

"How do you get them back from high places?" Christine asked Little K.

"Easy. Look."

The two elves went off the stage and returned with a tall, bare Christmas tree on a trolley. In a flash, like sparkling rainbow jet planes, all the lights flew from their decorating positions around the conference hall and almost fought with each other to get a good place on the tree. For a minute or two, the tree was a writhing mass of twinkling lights, its branches shaking and quivering at the onslaught. Then the lights seemed, by mutual agreement, to find a place of their own amongst the greenery and draped themselves beautifully.

"Awesome!" breathed Nick.

"Unbelievable," echoed Christine

"Formidable," came a garlic-laden comment from behind them.

There was a trickle of applause from the enthusiastic delegates but it was nothing like the approval they had shown when they first saw the lights.

"Ladies and Gentlemen." The Chairman spoke again. "I'm sure that I don't have to tell you that our conference is always organised so that we present the proposals on the first and second days, then we debate amongst ourselves, *in a civilised manner*, on the third and fourth days, and we vote on the fifth and final day. *Now* is not the time to debate this extraordinary invention. This matter will be brought up on day three, when you may all give your *considered opinions.*"

There was a general murmur of understanding and the Chairman moved on to the next item. "Proposal number two, from Belsnickle of Canada, that we choose an International Gift-Giving date."

There was a collective groan and Belsnickle looked embarrassed as he stood up to present his argument. As he droned on about the advantages of Christmas Gift-Giving falling on the same day in every country, Christine could see that half of the delegates were not listening. They had heard it all before and they were not going to vote in favour of it this year, or any other year. Christine wasn't paying attention either. She knew that the next proposal was Pa Kringle's and her heart was beginning to do back flips as she realised that everyone would be looking at her.

Belsnickle finished his half-hearted presentation and sat down again. There was no applause. St.Nicholas of Belgium rose and waited for the Chairman to give him permission to speak. Old Man Christmas gave a nod and the Belgian said firmly,

"Mr Chairman, ladies and gentlemen, this is the thirty fourth time that this proposal has been brought to the annual conference. It is time that the Dynasty put a stop to proposals being put forward again and again, that obviously have no chance of success."

Many of the delegates shouted "Hear, hear!" and "Definitely!".

The Chairman sighed. "If you are proposing a change to the Constitution, St.Nicholas, then you will have to submit it formally to the secretaries for inclusion on tomorrow's agenda."

The Belgian triumphantly waved a prepared piece of paper, which he gave to one of the tomte secretaries, then he sat down, looking pleased with himself. Several of the delegates gave him a small ripple of appreciative applause.

"Now," the Chairman continued, "next on the agenda is the proposal from Kriss Kringle of America."

Pa Kringle stood up and Christine could see that the piece of paper in his hand was fluttering a little. She crossed both her fingers and craned forward to look at the adult observation gallery, where the wives of the delegates were watching, but she couldn't see Ma.

"I wish to propose that the role of Gift Bringer can be passed on to a female child, if there is no male child within a family to take on the role." There. He'd said it. His voice had cracked a little but he had said it loud and clear. There was a moment's silence. A couple of male delegates coughed. Then, suddenly, the whole row of female Gift Bringers stood and loudly applauded and cheered. Christine saw Pa wince. This display of female solidarity was not, necessarily, going to help the cause. But, Christine reasoned, at least it had broken the silence.

The Chairman banged his gavel. Babbo Natale's hand was raised. The Chairman nodded and the Italian stood up. La Befana led a chorus of boos and hisses and the Chairman banged his gavel again. "Ladies! Please!" he said sternly.

Babbo Natale spoke. "Mr Chairman and delegates. I am sure that I speak for everyone when I say that we are all sympathetic to the situation of our American cousin. Having no son to pass the traditional role on to is a great sorrow for him to bear."

There were a few murmured "Shame," and "Pity," and Christine felt the hot flush of anger creep up her face.

"However," Babbo Natale continued "There is no precedent for this proposal. As everyone here knows, the accepted solution for such a predicament is for the daughter to marry and the son-in-law to take on the Gift Bringer's role in his adopted country..."

There were more hisses from the Female Gift Bringers and the Chairman's gavel came down forcefully. "I won't warn you again, ladies!" he said, trying to sound even more stern.

Babbo Natale smirked and continued once more. "This issue has been debated before, although it has never been formally brought to the Conference as a proposal. I'm sure we can all recall the predicament of The Star Man of Poland, who had no son and heir in 1782, and, similarly, Feliz Navidad of Uruguay in 1886. These situations were all remedied by marriage. Surely the same can be done again? After all, the rest of the delegates have more than enough sons between them to provide a suitable husband."

"It's so unfair," Christine muttered under her breath.

"There is also the question of the strength required to perform the Gift Bringer role." Babbo Natale's comment brought forth groans of disgust from the Female Gift Bringers, all of whom had been delivering gifts to children for centuries, without the need for any extra muscles.

"The Chair recognises St.Lucy of Switzerland." Old Man Christmas sounded surprised but not unpleasantly so. St. Lucy was always regarded as a voice of moderation in The Sisterhood.

St. Lucy rose. "Mr Chairman and delegates. Surely it is time that the Yule Dynasty moved forward into the new Millennium? All over the world, women are rising to positions in society that, previously, would have been unheard of. Many countries now have female Heads of State, many companies now have female chief executives. It is surely outmoded to persist in the tradition that any family that has no sons should marry their daughters off to a male Yule in order to fill the job of Gift Bringer?"

There were several loud, male, voices raised in support of this sentiment. Mostly, from the Scandinavians, with their long-held views on equality.

"And, Mr Chairman..." St. Lucy continued, buoyed up by the display of support, "The issue of strength for the job is surely a myth? In these days of technological advances, most jobs require skill rather than strength. Handling a reindeer team is no more difficult than handling a big, powerful racehorse and there are many women jockeys now who will tell you that they can do the job as well as, if not better, than the men. Anyway, some male Gift Bringers are abandoning traditional reindeer teams in favour of more modern modes of transport, is that not so Babbo Natale?"

This mischievous reference to the Italian's big red Ferrari drew some laughter from the body of delegates and Babbo Natale scowled in irritation.

"Thank you St.Lucy" the Chairman smiled benignly at her. "Kriss Kringle, it falls to you to make your presentation and then the matter will be closed until we debate it fully on the third day."

Pa Kringle nodded and was about to speak when a flurry of Black Gang in the corner of the hall interrupted proceedings. Two of them conferred urgently with Black Peter who, in turn, scuttled up to the podium and whispered in the Chairman's ear.

"One moment please..." Old Man Christmas looked alarmed and put his hand over the microphone. Pa Kringle stood, awkwardly, not sure whether to sit down again, darted a look back towards Christine and shrugged his shoulders.

"What is happening?" whispered Little K.

"I don't know," Christine replied.

The Chairman took his hand away from his microphone and said "Ladies and gentlemen, I apologise for this interruption, but there is an item on Sky News which concerns us all."

He motioned with his hand and the lights dimmed. The Curtains behind his head parted and a screen sputtered into life. The news anchorman was reading from his autocue with amusement.

"Yes folks, it's official today. Christmas has been banned in one town in England."

There was a collective intake of breath from the delegates.

"The town of Plinkbury in Whirr-sester-shire…"

"Woostersheer, you dope," muttered Nick, correcting the anchorman's pronounciation.

"…has officially cancelled Christmas. At a meeting yesterday, the Town Council decided that there will be no Christmas tree in the town square; no Christmas lights in the shops and no carol singers will be allowed to sing carols in the streets. Sounds like December in this town is going to be a pretty dismal affair. Our reporter in England, Jane Hoffmeyer, has the full story…"

The screen changed to a cold, wet day in an English town and the roving reporter was clutching a large umbrella and her microphone.

"Yes, that's correct Scott. I'm standing here in the town of Plinkbury, in the heart of rural England. It is official. Christmas will not be happening this year in this particular town. I have here the Leader of the Council, Angela Summer, who will explain to us her Council's decision. Angela, is this really true?"

A steely-eyed middle-aged woman appeared on screen. "Yes, Jane, it is quite true. The Plinkbury Council decided that because of issues of health and safety and out of respect to ethnic and religious minorities, that Christmas will not be endorsed in any way, shape or form in this town. In fact, the Council have gone further than that. We have passed a bye-law which gives us the power to fine any local shops that put up Christmas decorations."

Some of the Dynasty members shouted "Sacrilege!" and "Unbelievable!"

The reporter probed further. "If I may ask you, Angela, what are these health and safety concerns which have prompted this drastic action?"

"Well, firstly, the tall Christmas tree which the Council has traditionally funded in the town square, is a fire hazard. It requires power through a series of leads and transformers, which someone could easily trip over, and the lights themselves constitute a real threat of fire. Secondly, the street lights which the Council have also traditionally funded, cause traffic congestion when they are being put up and taken down and, also, congestion in the square when cars slow down to look at them. Also, the cost of running these lights for the whole of December is a very big drain on our budget."

"And the carol singers? How do they present a risk?"

"The Women's Institute Choral Society usually sings carols, alternating with the Salvation Army Band. The traditional location of these groups, on the Town Hall steps, is a direct contravention of fire regulations. Also, the Council feels that overtly Christian music is offensive to other religions."

"I see. But why fine individual shopkeepers if they display Christmas decorations? After all, it wouldn't cost the Council any money, if other people paid to put up some lights, would it?"

Ms. Summer's reply was terse. "Cost is not the issue, in this instance. It's a question of sensitivities. Rather than offend anyone, the Council felt that it would be better to ban the season altogether."

The reporter turned back to the camera. "Well, there you have it, Scott. Christmas is officially banned in Plinkbury. The question is, will other English towns follow suit? Pretty soon, England could find itself in the situation it was in in 1644 when Christmas was banned by the Puritans. This is Jane Hoffmeyer reporting for Sky News from the town of Plinkbury in England."

The screen went blank and everyone sat in shocked silence. Nick flushed with embarrassment as his father rose to his feet and spoke.

"I would like to apologise to the conference for this outrageous turn of events in England and assure the delegates that I had no idea that such a thing was going to happen."

Most delegates nodded and gave him looks of pity. Not since the old Soviet Union banned religion, and all its festivals, had the

Yule Dynasty been faced with such a calamitous event.

The Chairman banged his gavel. "In keeping with Section 24, Paragraph 12, Subsection 2 of the Yule Constitution, I now declare a State of Emergency. All previous items on the agenda will have to be set aside for an emergency debate. Ladies and gentlemen, we will reconvene after lunch to discuss this grave situation."

The Chairman swept out and the delegates trickled out after him, looking sombre. Pa Kringle kept shaking his head, while he gathered up his papers. So near and yet so far. He had been within a whisker of getting his proposal debated by the Dynasty and now he would have to wait another year.

Christmas was in danger.

☆

CHAPTER SIX

A Plan is Formed

Everything was in turmoil. Here it was – November 29th – and the Yule Conference was faced with a ban on Christmas. It was just in one small town in England but it could escalate. What was to be done?

The three teenagers and their perpetual shadow, Pere Noel Junior, who seemed to view his new friends as an endless source of food, wandered the corridors of the conference centre. Adults were huddled together in little groups, gravely debating the news.

The Secretariat, which was a large contingent of tomtes, based in offices on the ground floor, had swung into action on the telephones. They were calling in publicity favours from any media in England that had ever written or spoken favourably about Christmas. Soon, the television and radio networks would be buzzing with protests about the action of Plinkbury Council. Ms Angela Summer was going to disappear under a media onslaught, the like of which had never been seen in England since the last Royal Wedding.

After lunch, Christine and her friends returned to the conference chamber for a while but the Emergency Debate seemed to be going around in circles. Grandfather Frost of Russia spoke at length about the Communist regime in the USSR and counselled patience, saying that the people would keep Christmas alive in secret and it would resurface again. He would have spoken for longer but his mother told him, in no uncertain terms, to shut up and sit down.

At first, everyone blamed Santa of England for not doing more to promote Christmas. This made Nick really mad and Christine felt very sorry for her friend. Then St.Lucy of Switzerland stood up and told everyone off for being so unpleasant and made them all apologise to their English cousin, one by one. Santa of England responded graciously and said to everyone that he didn't see what more he could have done and everyone agreed that it really wasn't his fault.

The debate went on and on but the only positive decision that was made was to ask the toy manufacturers to put adverts in the English newspapers saying that Christmas was a wonderful thing and everyone should celebrate it. Other than that, the Yule Dynasty couldn't think of anything else. The Plinkbury Council's regulation, fining any displays of Christmas decorations, would come into effect, in two day's time, on December 1st. Time was running out.

That evening, the Kringle family sat around disconsolately. Pa was worn out from the endless debating in the conference chamber, Ma was depressed because the Kringle proposal had been swept away and Christine felt frustrated by everything. No-one felt like going down to dinner in the banqueting hall, so Ma whipped up some hot chocolate and broke out the toffee tin they had brought from home.

There was a knock at the door. Christine opened it and was amazed but pleased to see Nick and his father, standing awkwardly on the threshold, gifts in hand.

"Come in, come in," she said and called over her shoulder to her parents "Ma, Pa, it's my friend Nick and his father!"

Kriss Kringle looked surprised and rose to his feet, apologising for his lack of boots and jacket.

"Please" said Santa of England, proffering a bottle of British wine, "I can't wait to get out of the uniform when I get back to my room."

Ma was all welcoming smiles and urging the guests to sit. She busied herself with making some more hot chocolate and passing the toffee tin around. Nick smiled gratefully at Christine.

"I guess this is a difficult time for you." Pa Kringle was sympathetic towards his English cousin. Santa nodded and pulled a face.

"How is your wife taking it?" Ma said, without thinking, and then realised she had embarrassed everyone. There was a guilty silence. Santa of England had been avoided socially by most of the Yule Dynasty for many years, simply because he had married a tall elf.

"She's not here, of course" replied Santa, clearing his throat. "She had some family commitments. But I have spoken to her on the telephone and she is very concerned."

There was another awkward silence. Ma, in particular, felt ashamed. In her heart of hearts she knew that all the wives were a little jealous of Mrs Santa of England, who was extremely beautiful and willowy, as elves were, whereas the majority of Yule women were round and homely. They had all been distant, the first time they had all met her, and she felt remorseful.

"You have such a lovely son!" she said brightly, in an effort to make amends.

Santa smiled with relief, Nick looked at the floor and Christine laughed.

The ice was broken and Pa cracked open the bottle of British wine. "Not bad!" he said, rolling it around his tongue like a professional wine taster. "Almost as good as our Californian wines."

Ma chortled and slapped him on the back. "Hark at him! He wouldn't know a Gluhwein from a Chablis, if it bit him on the bottom!"

Everyone laughed at that and settled back to bask in the warm glow of new-found friendship.

There was some pleasant chit-chat, mostly about their children and what they were doing at school, then Santa's face clouded and he turned the conversation to the current emergency state.

"I feel very responsible for what has happened in Plinkbury," he confided.

"You shouldn't!" said Pa sympathetically. "It's not your fault at all."

"All the same, imagine if this had happened in your country."

Pa reflected for a moment and realised that he would feel devastated if an American town had taken the same action as Plinkbury.

"My son," Santa continued "has ventured a suggestion which might solve both of our problems."

"*Both* problems?" Pa was puzzled.

"Well, yes. The situation regarding your daughter and the Gift Bringer's job."

Pa was curious. "Go ahead."

Santa turned to his son and nodded encouragingly. Nick took a deep breath and began to outline his plan.

"I propose that Christine and I, together with Little K and his lights, travel to Plinkbury to start a resistance movement in the town. We can encourage the people to rebel against this stupid bye law and we can decorate the town with K's lights. They have no discernible power source and no-one will have to pay for the electricity."

Pa smiled and looked bemused. Nick continued.

"If we are successful in getting Christmas re-instated, we can say that it was all Christine's efforts and that will give her plenty of credit with the Yule Conference."

"And..." Christine chimed in excitedly, "It would show how valuable Little K's lights are in emergency situations!"

Ma and Pa looked proudly at their considerate daughter. She's always thinking of others, thought Ma, and felt as though she was about to start crying.

Pa, as always, thought of the disadvantages of a situation. "Have you spoken to Santa Kurohsu about this?"

Santa of England looked at Nick. "My son thought that you

and I could persuade him."

"Mmm..." Pa stroked his beard thoughtfully. "We can't let the youngsters go to England unsupervised."

"Pa!" Christine was scornful. "We're not babies!"

"Your father's right," Ma jumped to her husband's defence. "I know you think you're grown up but you're only fourteen. And you're proposing to travel to another country on your own! I don't think so!"

Santa intervened before Ma got herself too wound up. "My wife will look after them. As we speak, she is booking two rooms in a bed and breakfast facility in Plinkbury."

"We...ell" Ma was slightly reassured, then she had a thought. "Perhaps I could go as well?"

"No!" Everyone spoke at once and Ma looked rather shocked, and a little hurt, at their vehemence. Christine felt guilty that she did not want her mother to spoil her big adventure. Pa patted Ma's hand, sensing that she felt a bit rejected.

"Honey, you can't leave the conference, it would be noticed." He spoke in a practical manner and that seemed to make Ma feel better. "If this thing is going to be done, it has to be done quietly, with no one here suspecting that it is being done. If you understand what I mean." He had got himself tied up in knots a bit.

"What your husband means..." Santa continued "Is that the teenagers will not be missed. *You* would be missed. I'm sorry to say this, but we don't want the Dynasty involved in this venture. If they know about it, they will insist that it is debated and ratified before anything can be done, by which time, it will be too late. We have to act *now*." He was quite firm and Ma nodded in compliance.

"You're right!" Pa started pulling on his boots. "Let's go and see our Japanese cousin and sort this out." He was energised by doing something positive. Action was Pa Kringle's middle name.

"Ma," he said, barking orders like a commander, "while the menfolk make the plans, you can help us by getting these two youngsters organised and packed."

"Can't we come with you, Pa?" Christine didn't like being relegated to women's work. Packing suitcases was no fun.

"No honey. I know Santa Kurohsu quite well. This needs to be man to man."

With that, the two men left with a purpose and Ma's eyes narrowed.

"We're going to do more than pack, Christine. Don't you worry."

Christine smiled, sensing rebellion in Ma's tone of voice. She winked at Nick. "What did you have in mind, Ma?" she whispered gleefully.

"Honey, get on that phone and gather The Sisterhood. Tell them to get here as fast as they can. I'll whip up some egg-nog and draw up the battle plans."

"What's your mother up to?" Nick whispered nervously to Christine, when Ma had left the room.

Christine laughed softly. "I don't know. But if The Sisterhood are involved, you can bet it will be good!"

"I like it," said La Befana, as she sipped her egg nog, but she wasn't talking about the drink, she was giving her seal of approval to Nick's plan and Ma's additions to the plan. Christine was looking at her mother through fresh eyes. She had no idea that her mother could be so devious.

Ma continued, "So, ladies, we're all agreed on what we have to do?"

The assembled Sisterhood nodded eagerly. Santa Lucia of Sicily recapped the plan. "St Lucy, French Tante Arie and St. Lucia are going to make the banners. Befana, Babushka, Canadian Tante Arie and I are going to stir up the conference hall tomorrow."

"Right." Ma beamed with pleasure.

"And we are going to organise some vandalism." Christine was referring to herself, Nick and Little K.

"This is like a master stroke from the great Italian strategist, Machiavelli," La Befana looked triumphant. "Distract the enemy, take the enemies' assets and conquer!"

"Er…quite." Ma looked a little apprehensive. La Befana could be a loose cannon at times. It wouldn't do for her to get carried away and spoil things. "But we must proceed cautiously."

"Pah!" Befana said contemptuously. "Caution is for the faint-hearted. You have asked me to keep the delegates distracted at tomorrow's conference and this I shall do. They shall have a debate to end all debates. Nothing else shall occupy their minds."

"OK." Ma was still not sure but she gave a hesitant smile of reassurance to Christine. "I hope you kids can pull off your part of the plan."

"Don't worry Ma. We know what to do." Christine and Nick looked positive and Ma nodded.

By the time Pa Kringle and Santa of England got back to the Kringle suite it was past midnight. The Sisterhood had long gone – not to their beds but about their secret work. Nick and Christine were asleep in separate chairs, waiting for their respective fathers.

"Did you persuade him?" Ma whispered, hovering anxiously.

Pa nodded wearily. "It took some work. Old Santa Kurohsu would have nothing to do with it at first. You know the Japanese. Very honourable. Didn't want to upset anyone. But we talked him round, in the end. Are the kids all packed?"

"Of course." After The Sisterhood had left, Ma had whirled around the suite like a maniac, getting Christine's things together. Christine, meanwhile, had gone round to Nick's room to help him pack and they had only recently returned.

"I'd better get Nick back to his own bed," said Santa softly, shaking his son's shoulder. Nick looked up at him with bleary eyes. "Come on, son. Let's get you to bed and then I'd better go and feed the reindeer, ready for your journey tomorrow." Pa and Santa had decided that the smaller English sleigh, with its four reindeer would be easiest for Nick to handle on the journey to England.

Ma said nothing. She knew there were other plans afoot, that were best kept to themselves. The men would only worry. She had learnt, through long experience, the woman's trick of only telling men what they *needed* to know. Too much detail and they started spoiling things.

Santa and Nick left and Pa Kringle gently raised Christine to her feet.

"Time for bed, honey."

Christine stumbled, on auto pilot, to her room and climbed under the duvet, barely registering the change of sleeping quarters, and was soon deeply asleep.

"We've got ourselves one brave girl there, Ma." Pa put his arm around his wife and looking at Christine's sleeping head.

"We certainly have, Pa. Now come to bed, we have a busy day tomorrow."

As he lay in the dark, listening to Ma snoring, due to the effects of too much egg nog, Pa hoped he would cope with the repercussions of going behind the Dynasty's collective back and taking this unauthorised action. If it didn't succeed, the fallout could be alarming.

Still, he thought, turning over on to his side and sighing, as sleep continued to elude him, what's the worst they can do? They could bar him from the family conferences but that would be no great loss. If he never had to attend another Yule Dynasty Conference he would be a very happy man. And with that thought, he sank into a blissful sleep, with a smile on his lips.

☆

CHAPTER SEVEN

Mayhem and Larceny

The next day, everyone was very nervous. Pa Kringle felt a knot in his stomach which almost, but not quite, prevented him from eating his breakfast chocolate brownies. Nevertheless, he would probably have indigestion all day.

Christine had already breakfasted and disappeared by the time he got up. Ma said she was just off to see her friends.

"Well I hope I see her sometime today, before she goes," Pa said, with a tinge of annoyance in his voice. Secretly, he was envious of his daughter's approaching adventure. He would much rather be out "saving Christmas" than stuck in a conference hall.

"What time is sunset again?" he asked Ma for the sixth time.

"Pa, for goodness sake, I told you. It's 2.30 in the afternoon. It gets dark really early in Finland in November. But the kids are not going to set off until 3.30 to make sure that they arrive in England after dark."

"I don't know. If the reindeer make good time, they could be in England in half an hour."

"Yes, I know. Don't worry about it Pa. Just stick to the plan." Ma knew that the kids would be in England a lot faster than Pa estimated but she said nothing.

Christine and Nick had gone to fetch Little K. His father opened the door and smiled. "My son is ready," he announced, ushering them into the room. Little K appeared, looking flushed and excited, carrying a holdall. Christine hugged him. Nick just nodded sheepishly.

Santa Kurohsu spoke. "I thank you both for this opportunity to restore honour to the Kurohsu family," and he bowed deeply.

"Sure," said Nick.

"You're very welcome," said Christine.

Little K bowed to his father and Santa Kurohsu laid his hand on his son's head and murmured a few words in Japanese. Little K bowed again and the three friends left.

"What did your father say to you?" Christine was always curious – or, as Ma preferred to call it - nosy.

"He gave me his blessing and said I must be careful not to shame our ancestors," said Little K gravely.

"Cool." Nick couldn't think of anything else to say.

Christine was excited. Her cheeks were pink and she had a permanent smile on her face. "K, we need to tell you about the plan," she said breathlessly.

"What plan is this, please?" Little K asked hesitantly because it sounded to him as though things could get complicated.

"Trust us." Christine was firm. "We know what we're doing."

Pere Noel Junior was sitting disconsolately in the teenage viewing gallery. He had hoped that the other three would be there, with some food for him. His mother kept trying to put him on a diet and this morning's breakfast had been woefully inadequate. One croissant, no butter and sugar free jam, a glass of fruit juice and an apple. A growing lad, with an appetite such as his, could not exist on such a pathetic meal. His mother had decided that the Pere Noel family would, like the Kringle family, breakfast in their rooms, so there would be no danger of her son gorging himself on the breakfast buffet laid out in the banqueting hall. Then she had marched him through the complex and pushed him into the viewing gallery with instructions to stay put until lunchtime, when she would collect him and feed him a little soup and a roll. His stomach rumbled with hunger.

Meanwhile, Christine, Nick and Little K were passing the giant

Christmas tree. The members of The Sisterhood were dotted about the foyer. Eyes met, heads nodded and watches were synchronised. It was time to put Operation Save Christmas into action.

Little K had been fully briefed, and was feeling a little apprehensive, but he set off with Nick in the direction of the transport hangar. St.Lucy of Switzerland followed them, at a discreet distance. Christine made for the banqueting hall and the breakfast buffet. The rest of The Sisterhood, carrying suspicious looking bundles, gathered together, ready to enter the conference hall.

Everything had to be timed to perfection.

In the transport hangar, the animals were dozing fitfully in their stalls, having been fed their early morning snack. Rows of sleighs, carriages and carts gleamed faintly in the low lighting. Giving all the transport a wash and wax job was one of the complimentary services given by the tomtes of the host country. However, one mode of transport did not just gleam, it positively dazzled and shone - its sleek curves reflecting the light from the overhead lamps. Babbo Natale's red Ferrari. Sitting beside the powerful car, also dozing, like the animals, was a large Italian elf, dressed in an Armani suit and expensive Gucci loafers. What style! Nick thought both car and elf were awesome. He peered at his reflection in the glass-like wing of the car.

"Hey kid!" the elf had woken from his doze. "Keep away from the boss's car!"

"I was just admiring it," Nick said, holding his hands up as though he had a gun pointed at him. "My friend and I think this car is awesome."

"Yes, awesome," echoed Little K, smiling happily.

"It's a 360 Modena, right?" Nick peered into the interior.

"Nah," the elf replied scornfully. "It's a 360 Modena Challenge. The racing version of the Modena. The boss had it specially made."

"Double awesome!" Nick was genuinely impressed.

Little K chipped in to the conversation, displaying his

encyclopaedic knowledge of cars. "But the same V8 mid engine with 85 millimetre bore, 79 millimetre stroke, 11 compression ratio, double variable valve timing, camshaft and five valves per cylinder? Yes?"

"Ah...but..." the elf warmed to the two boys. He liked car enthusiasts, so he proceeded to outline the finer points of the heightened compression ratio, the maximum power and torque. Nick winked at Little K. So far so good. Pretty soon, they would persuade the Ferrari's minder to let them sit in the car whilst he showed them how it actually worked.

Christine, meanwhile, was entering the banqueting hall. Her eyes scanned the lavish buffet. Few delegates were still at breakfast. It was almost time for the Emergency Debate to start and most of them had finished and hurried off. There were just a few wives, gossiping in a little knot at a far table. Christine spotted what she needed – a very large and completely untouched blueberry pie. She deftly scooped the platter up and exited, grabbing a napkin on the way, which she draped over the pie.

Weaving in and out of the throngs of delegates making for the conference hall, she made her way up to the teenage viewing gallery. As she expected, there was Pere Noel Junior, sitting alone, looking forlorn. His eyes lit up when he saw her and she smiled.

"I have something for you" she said, whisking the napkin off of the pie. The French boy's face broke into a wide grin. "But..." she added quickly. "You can't eat it here. Someone might come in. Come with me."

He nodded eagerly and followed her without hesitation.

St.Lucy had slipped into the transport hangar, unnoticed, and proceeded to quietly offer the Swiss horses some pieces of apple. They nuzzled her gratefully and she stroked their noses. Over by the Ferrari, the elf was talking animatedly about his boss' wonderful car and she waited patiently. Then, the elf opened the car door and beckoned the two boys inside. That meant it was time for her to move. She gave the horses one final pat and left, heading for the administration offices.

The conference hall doors had opened, and grave delegates were filing in. Kriss Kringle shot a glance at his English cousin. It was going to be a long morning. Ma had told him not to worry about things and just get on with business.

"The kids are not leaving until after lunch, so just concentrate on the Emergency Debate, Pa," she had said to him. Ma was always practical, and usually calm, but it seemed to her husband that she had been a little jittery this morning. He decided that she must be finding it hard to let her only child go off on such an adventure.

Once all the delegates were in and the chairman and his secretaries had taken up their positions, the doors were closed. Old Man Christmas took a deep breath and silently prayed that this morning would proceed without too much argument. But his prayer was in vain. At that moment there was a flurry of movement from the three rows of Female Gift Bringers and they produced three large banners.

In a state of shock, the delegates stared at the banners – and the defiant faces of the women holding them.

...said Banner number one.

...said Banner number two.

...was number three.

The conference hall exploded into a barrage of shouts, catcalls and outrage. Old Man Christmas buried his face in his hands and vowed that he would *never* host another Yule Dynasty conference as long as he lived.

Downstairs in The Secretariat, the elves and tomtes were frantically busy. They were all on the telephone, engaged in what was called "damage limitation." In other words they were still trying to stir the worldwide media up into defending Christmas from the potentially fatal actions of Plinkbury Council. St. Lucy entered, a note in her hand, and hovered, waiting to get some attention.

"May I help you?" A tomte said, from the region of her elbow. Lucy jumped.

"Er, yes. Em… Babbo Natale wants this message taken to his chauffeur in the transport hangar. I would take it myself but I'm already late for the conference."

"Of course," the elf said smoothly. "Leave it to me."

The note was taken and a tomte was despatched to deliver it. Lucy gave a small sigh of relief and hurried off to sneak into the conference hall.

As she crept in, the noise was deafening. OzNick was on his feet, shouting something about being sick of the interference of

"Sheilas" and Old Man Christmas was banging his gavel in vain.

"How's it going?" Lucy shouted to La Befana, as she slid into her seat.

"Magnifico!" Befana shouted back with glee, pausing only to make the sign of the evil eye at OzNick before he sat down. "Watch this!" she added as she leapt to her feet. "I have the backing of his Holiness the Pope on this issue!" she shouted triumphantly and the massed Kings of South America leapt to their feet and applauded.

Black Peter forcefully blew his whistle and the conference hall subsided into resentful murmurings.

"As the Female Gift Bringers have come to this conference determined to force their opinions on to the agenda – we will debate each of those…" he waved his hands at the banners "…those…issues…one at a time – **IN A CIVILISED MANNER!**" His voice rose to a shout and he managed to achieve total silence in the auditorium. Mopping his brow with a handkerchief, he continued "La Befana, you will please present the first statement…" he could hardly bring himself to state it, "… that Men Have Ruined Christmas."

La Befana rose to her feet, glorying in the fact that she was now going to spend the best part of the next hour speaking on her favourite topic.

In the transport hangar, Christine stood in the shadows, restraining a salivating Pere Noel Junior, while she watched the tomte arrive with the message. He knocked on the windscreen of the Ferrari and the elf minder got out and read the note. He motioned the boys out of the car and Christine hoped that he was asking them to mind the Ferrari while he was gone. After he left with the tomte, Christine beamed at Nick and Little K.

"Everything's working perfectly," said Nick happily.

"Now," Christine said, turning to the French boy, who was almost in tears at being so near and yet so far from the massive blueberry pie, "you sit in the car and eat your pie and we'll stand here and keep watch."

Boy and pie were loaded into the car and the friends decided to avert their eyes from the carnage that was about to take place. They had learnt, after only a short acquaintance with Pere Noel Junior, that when he ate it was not a pretty sight.

"So, do you guys know how to drive this thing now?" Christine asked, nodding in the direction of the Ferrari.

"Absolutely," Nick was trembling with excitement.

"Piece of cake," Little K added happily. "I could even take it apart and put it back together again, if necessary."

"Good. Now we just have to wait for the minder to return and hope we can pull it off," said Christine, crossing her fingers.

Guido, Babbo Natale's elf-minder-chauffeur was panting a little as he raced towards the conference hall. He was a good-natured elf. Very strong but a little slow. He knew about cars but very little else. He couldn't imagine why the boss had sent the note but it was not for him to question.

A tomte opened the conference hall door quietly and put a finger to her lips. Guido nodded and slid silently into the hall, making his way around the perimeter.

Babbo Natale was exhausted and very irritable. La Befana was only halfway through her speech on men and Christmas and how the one had ruined the other. She had just started on her favourite topic – aimed at him – on how certain male Gift Bringers had forged alliances with certain toy manufacturers and were making toys unnecessarily expensive. In a moment she was going to talk about certain Gift Bringers who had abandoned traditional forms of transport in favour of flashy modern cars, which ruined the image of Gift Bringers for young children. Then she would probably mention the fact that a certain Gift Bringer had had ten million Christmas cards made last year, showing him sitting in his bright red Ferrari.

Guido tapped his boss on the shoulder and Babbo Natale looked at him and frowned.

"What is it?" he hissed.

Guido looked puzzled and showed him the note. Babbo Natale

scanned it.

It said, *I need to see you. The Boss.*

"It's not from me!" he hissed at Guido "It's not my handwriting. They must have given this note to you by mistake. Must be from some other delegate."

Guido nodded. He opened his mouth to point out that the note was in Italian and no-one else would write a note in Italian but Babbo Natale waved him away impatiently, so he shrugged his shoulders and left.

La Befana was now reading out a list of the most-asked-for gifts of the last ten years. Statistics proved, she said, that male Gift Bringers were promoting toys for boys that were much more expensive than the toys for girls. And, what was more disgraceful, she continued, boys were not being encouraged to ask for books in their Christmas stockings. Just because *certain* male Gift Bringers hadn't read a book in years, did not mean that they should pass on their bad habits to the younger generations. And so it went on. Babbo Natale began to feel sick.

When Guido got back to the transport hangar, he smiled to see that the boys were still there, but his smile faded when he saw that they had been joined by a girl and all three of them looked very worried.

"What's wrong?" he said fearfully.

The children parted, all apologising at once.

"We couldn't stop him…"

"We didn't realise…"

"It all happened so quickly…"

Guido peered into the car. He couldn't see inside properly because there appeared to be blue, sticky stuff all over the window. He opened the door and screamed.

There was a large boy – at least he thought it was a boy, but his face was blue and covered in crumbs – who smiled hesitantly at him. The boy's clothes were stained with blue and the whole of the interior of his Boss's beloved Ferrari was spattered with blueberry syrup, sugar and pieces of crust. The boy tried to speak but only succeeded in dribbling a large amount of blueberry syrup over the front of his t-shirt and on to the gear stick. Guido reached out a hand to grab the boy but, just at that moment, due to a piece of pie crust getting lodged in his windpipe, Pere Noel Junior had a fit of coughing which sprayed wet pastry and squashed blueberries over the front of Guido's suit and sunglasses.

Guido screamed again. A little longer this time, with a poignant note of despair.

The French boy looked as though he was going to burst into tears. "Je m'excuse…" he gargled through his emerging tears. Christine rushed to his side and reassured him. She felt guilty about the fact that they had used him. He was a nice boy really.

Guido snapped and let forth a stream of Italian swear words. At least they all assumed they were swear words. He was ranting and raving, kicking the tyres of the car and making all the animals in their stalls rear up in fear.

Finally and dramatically he announced "I shall kill myself!" and all the children said "No, no," in a sort-of there-there voice and proceeded to calm him down.

"We'll clean the car," offered Nick, as he grabbed Guido's arm.

"We'll make it as good as new," promised Little K, grabbing the other arm.

"You won't even know that anything happened," added Christine, as she hauled Pere Noel Junior out of the car to an upright position.

Guido calmed down and then he started to panic again. "What if the Boss comes down here? He sometimes comes down here to talk to his car…" His voice trailed off in embarrassment and Christine sniggered. Gift Bringers came down here to talk to their animals and reassure them, but whoever heard of a grown man talking to his car? Then she looked at the faces of the boys, who seemed to find the statement perfectly reasonable, and she sighed.

Nick put a friendly arm around the distraught Italian. "We'll take the car to another building and clean it. It may take us a few days."

"A few days!" Guido looked horrified.

"I have a special Japanese cleaning fluid," said Little K reassuringly, "but it must be applied once every twenty four hours. We will do three applications, maybe. Get rid of all the stains. The car will be as good as new again."

"What am I going to tell the Boss?" Guido looked helpless.

"Tell him the car has gone for special tune-up and wax job. Tell him it was a free offer. Tell him the car will come back better than ever." Little K was very persuasive.

Guido looked at the little Japanese boy and hope flickered in his eyes.

"We'll take the car away and we promise to return it as good as new," said Nick giving the elf minder a slap on the back. Guido nodded. For the moment he was a broken man. For an Italian to witness the desecration of a Ferrari was a trauma that only several glasses of wine could erase. He turned on his heel to find the nearest bar.

"I'll tell the Boss that the car will be away for three days, " he said over his shoulder as he departed, "and if you can't put the car right, you'd better start praying, because we'll all be dead meat."

The teenagers looked at each other and smiled. Phase One of the plan was completed. Phase Two was about to begin.

☆

CHAPTER EIGHT

Phase Two

Christine needed to take Pere Noel Junior off to get him cleaned up but not before they had made use of his considerable strength to help them push the Ferrari into the boiler room, next to the transport hangar. Once the car was safely hidden away, everyone scattered in different directions.

Christine took the French boy to the Kringle suite, where Ma was ready with soap and flannel and stain remover. Pere Noel Junior was scrubbed and rubbed and his clothes were washed and hung over the radiators to dry. Meanwhile he was dressed in a pair of Pa Kringle's large pyjamas and Ma fed him gingerbread and hot chocolate to keep him quiet.

"You run along honey," she whispered to Christine. "I can look after the boy until his clothes are dry."

With a backward look at her happily munching French cousin, Christine slipped out of the door and made her way back to the boiler room, taking her luggage with her.

Meanwhile, Nick and Little K had popped backstage at the conference hall to retrieve the large basket on wheels which contained the magic lights. The noise from the hall was phenomenal. Some male Gift bringer was shouting "You have no grasp of the business realities of Christmas!" accompanied by a chorus of "Hear! Hear!" and "Absolutely!" Then a female Gift Bringer was shouting back "Business realities!?! I understand fraud when I see it!" The conference hall erupted into more shouts and catcalls. Nick raised his eyebrows at Little K and they shook their heads at the folly of adults.

The three friends met up at the car and proceeded to load all the luggage and the squirming lights into the vast emptiness of its trunk.

"Have you got any more lights?" Nick enquired, licking his fingers. Flipping the lever inside the car, to open the trunk, had been a sticky business.

Little K nodded. "Yes. Back in my room. I shall fetch them. And also the miracle Japanese upholstery cleaner."

As he disappeared, three of The Sisterhood arrived, clutching bundles.

"The conference has adjourned for lunch," said St.Lucy gleefully. "It's been such fun this morning!"

"I heard," said Nick drily. "Did any fist fights break out?"

"Almost!" said Babushka, chuckling. "When I was giving my speech about the religious side of Christmas being abandoned in favour of commercialism, there was a sort of fight between the Three Kings and Papa Noel of Spain. Mind you, they've been fighting for the last ten years over who should really be the Gift Bringers in their country."

"Here are the banners we've made – what do you think?" Tante Arie unrolled the bundles on the floor.

Christine and Nick stood over them and were duly impressed.

said the first banner

said the second banner

said the third.

The banners were beautifully made out of fabric and, here and there, The Sisterhood had sewn twinkling stars, hearts and holly leaves.

"They're wonderful!" breathed Christine. It must have taken you all night to sew these!"

The three women looked pleased. "Well. Many hands make light work, you know. In fact we made six banners altogether. Three for the conference hall and three for you," explained Tante Arie.

"Excellent!" Nick started rolling them up carefully and putting them in the car boot.

Little K returned, carrying a large hockey bag in one hand and a spray cleaner in the other. The movement of the hockey bag told everyone that more lights were inside.

"Well. We must away and grab a bite of lunch," St Lucy was very excited. "Then it's back to the fray!"

"So far we're only halfway through presenting our concerns about Christmas," Babushka added. "All the delegates have been so fired up by it all that they haven't had time to think about the Plinkbury problem. There have been no pauses for news broadcasts or anything."

"Befana thinks that she can keep the arguments raging all through tomorrow as well!" Tante Arie chuckled. "By the time anyone pauses for breath, you children will have started your work in England."

"Good luck little ones." St Lucy gave each of them a big hug and dabbed a handkerchief to her eyes as she left.

"I'd better go and say goodbye to my father before he finishes lunch," said Christine. "You boys should see your fathers too."

"I have said my goodbyes," said Little K. "I shall stay here and clean the car."

"Oh you can't do it all on your own!" Christine said with concern.

"No, it's fine. You go."

In the Kringle suite, Pa was pacing up and down in front of Ma. He was fuming – an egg and cress sandwich in one hand and a glass of mulled wine in the other.

"You'll get terrible heartburn," said Ma, trying to keep a straight face.

"I can't help it!" Pa was beside himself. "Now Ma, I know that those women are your friends but they have stirred up a hornet's nest and no mistake! Do you know that Belsnickle and I found ourselves on the receiving end of some very nasty accusations?"

"Oh?" said Ma, feigning concern. "Like what, dear?"

"Like the fact that we, allegedly, have ignored the religious side of Christmas and …and these are Babushka's very words…turned everybody in North America and Canada into worshippers of the almighty dollar."

"Oh dear!" Ma felt guilty. It hadn't been part of the plan to make Pa Kringle look bad.

He took an angry bite of his sandwich. "And, of course, under the rules of the conference, I'm not allowed to reply properly until that pack of old biddies has finished!"

"Well what would you like to say to them, Pa, by way of reply, as it were?" Ma tried to calm her husband down.

Kriss Kringle stopped pacing for a moment and thought carefully. His voice dropped from a rant to a reasonable tone.

" I would say to them that just as Thanksgiving unites all the different people in America, from all their different backgrounds, into one celebration of being "American", then Christmas, now, in the 21st century, unites everyone in a celebration of love and peace, a celebration of light in the dark winter and in the joy of giving. Of course, it started out as a Christian ceremony, but, over the centuries, other faiths have taken the spirit of Christmas into their hearts without, necessarily embracing Christianity. I know Christmas has changed a lot and that people spend far too much money on presents. Sometimes I miss the days when children made little handmade tokens for their parents and, in turn, parents gave their children one big present, which meant so much more than the dozens of presents they get nowadays. I also miss the days when I went down chimneys and left an apple, an orange, some sweets, some nuts and some small toys in their stockings. But, I suppose, you can't turn the clock back. I just know that, underneath it all, the spirit of Christmas is still there and maybe that's what we should concentrate on. We should be spreading more Christmas cheer, encouraging the unselfish side of Christmas and making people think about what they can do for others at Christmas time, instead of only thinking of themselves."

His voice had got softer and softer and Ma's eyes were shining with pride. Suddenly, they were both shocked by the sound of one person applauding. Christine had come into the room, at the beginning of her father's speech, and had listened, with great astonishment, as he crystallised his thoughts.

"Write it down Pa; write it down *now*, while you remember it," she urged him.

Kriss nodded. Yes, of course. It would make the perfect speech for tomorrow. He pushed the last piece of sandwich in his mouth and rushed into the bedroom to start writing.

"I want to take a copy of that speech with me to England," Christine said softly to Ma.

Ma nodded and gave her a big motherly hug.

"You will be careful, won't you?" she whispered anxiously to her daughter.

"Yes, Ma. Don't worry. Nick's mother will be looking after us. It's going to be a great adventure."

"Of course it is." Ma tried to sound positive.

Half an hour later, Christine was on her way back to the boiler room, clutching a bag of food her mother had put together. Ma would be following on with a photocopy of Pa's speech.

Nick had arrived back too and was helping Little K finish off the rehabilitation of the Ferrari. Christine was invited to inspect it and she pronounced it, "very clean indeed."

All was ready and the three of them climbed inside. The dashboard looked to Christine like the inside of a spaceship.

"You're sure you know how to fly this thing?" she asked Nick anxiously.

"Piece of cake!" He grinned at her and put the gear lever into neutral and started the engine. There was a faint purr – hardly audible at all. "This is one classy car," he said approvingly.

A panting Ma Kringle hammered on the side window. Nick pressed a button and the glass slid down effortlessly.

"Here's the speech!" she gasped, sticking a sheet of paper through the window to her daughter. "Now don't forget to put on your jumpers when you land. And your raincoats. It's raining in England."

"As usual," Nick suddenly felt depressed at the thought of England in November.

"Don't fuss, Ma," Christine said kindly, "Just open the doors for us."

Ma Kringle nodded and puffed her way over to the large double doors. As she swung them open, they could see that there was a snowstorm outside and she was struggling to keep the doors open.

"I'll go and help her," said Little K, slipping out of the front passenger seat. "You drive the car outside and wait for me."

Little K pushed the right hand door open fully and Ma braced herself against the left hand door. Nick released the clutch, slightly depressed the accelerator and the Ferrari glided smoothly out into the raging snow. Little K fought against the blizzard to close his door, then he struggled into the car, bringing half a ton of snow in with him.

Christine peered out the back window at Ma. She was almost completely covered in snowflakes but she bravely waved and blew a kiss. "Be careful!" she mouthed and Christine blew a kiss back. The door closed and Ma was gone.

Christine felt a lump in her throat. She'd never been away from her parents before – except for the brief spell at boarding school, which she had hated. Tears pricked at the back of her eyes.

"Here we go!" said Nick excitedly. "Fasten your seat belts!"

Little K and Christine scrabbled for their belts as Nick selected the cruise control button, put the car into F gear (F for Flying) and jammed down hard on the accelerator. The car shot forward and upwards, like a jet plane, and the three of them were thrown backwards into their seats. Nick flipped down a black cover to reveal an altimeter and threw a switch on the side of the steering wheel, which disengaged the wheel so that it could be pushed forwards and backwards as well as rotated. Chrsitine watched as the altimeter went round and round.

"I'm going to level off at twenty thousand feet and switch to autopilot," Nick announced. He sounded very sure of himself but twenty thousand feet sounded awfully high to Christine.

"It's a twenty minute flight on this course. I don't think there's any need to switch the car to hyperspeed," said Nick to Little K.

Little K agreed. Christine asked what hyperspeed was and the Japanese boy began to blind her with science.

"Sorry, I don't understand," she said, after Little K's lecture.

Nick laughed. "Basically, the car goes so fast it goes into a time warp, just like the reindeer do on Christmas Eve."

"Oh of course. Why didn't you say that?" she looked at Little K with exasperation. Every Yule knew that the Gift Bringers moved through the sky faster than the speed of light, when they had to deliver their gifts. How else would they get round a whole country in one night?

"After twenty minutes we'll make our descent to England. K's worked out the flight plan." Nick smiled reassuringly at Christine and she managed a watery smile back.

Little K unfolded a sheet on which he had made all kinds of calculations. "My best subject – air traffic control," he said happily.

"Thank God!" replied Christine, with feeling, as it was her

worst subject. In fact, last semester, the Senior Elf Traffic Controller had given her a C grade for all her work. Pa had said that some private tutoring might be in order, if she was really going to take over the USA's Gift Bringer job.

Nick flipped another switch, took both hands off the wheel and smiled again. "Now we can relax for twenty minutes. Next stop, England."

The friends gave each other anxious but happy looks. Operation Save Christmas was truly underway.

☆

CHAPTER NINE

The Amazing Zazu and Egan

In the middle of a small field in rural Yorkshire, Mrs Santa Claus of England and her brother, Egan, were sticking garden lights on poles into the ground, in the shape of a giant Christmas tree. This was to give Nick and his friends a landing guide.

The task was hampered somewhat by the fact that Zazu Claus was wearing stiletto heels and they kept sticking into the ground. Egan sighed. His sister was so ditzy. Breathtakingly beautiful, but ditzy.

"Zazu, why didn't you put on some boots? This is going to take us all night at this rate!"

Zazu giggled. "I know. I just didn't think. There was too much to concentrate on. These are my best designer shoes too."

Egan sighed again. "You go and stand over there. I'll finish off."

"OK, sweet pea." She brushed her long blonde hair out of her emerald green eyes and pecked him on the cheek. Then her brother watched as she teetered to the side of the field, occasionally stopping to pull her stiletto out of the soft mud.

Egan finished sticking the lights in the ground and went over to join his sister. She smiled adoringly at him and he shook his head in exasperation. If Zazu had also been blessed with brains she would be the most devastating female elf in the world. Everyone adored her because she was so beautiful and kind – not a malicious bone in her body – but she was also, and it pained Egan to think this of his own sister, unbelievably dumb.

To other elves, Zazu was walking proof that tall elves were inferior, that there was something abnormal about them. Some elves chose to believe the legend that tall elves were the result of intermarriage with humans. But Egan had done a great deal of research into the matter and he knew that tall elves were simply a genetic blip. A mutation within the species of elf. Egan suspected that tall elves were actually a throwback to the time, before man, when supernatural beings, such as elves, pixies, tomtes, leprechauns and so on, were thought to have been taller and, with the advent of man, they had diminished in size, so that they could hide more easily. But still, regular short elves continued to regard tall elves as stupid. Whenever elves told jokes, they were always about dumb tall elves.

This made Egan really irritable because he was probably more intelligent than the entire elf population put together. After enduring a childhood of simmering prejudice, he had opted out of the Yule Dynasty set-up, where tall elves were generally given inferior, boring jobs, and had struck out on his own. He now ran the all-year-round Christmas Shop on the south coast of England and an import and export business. He'd even been to a plastic surgeon in New York and had his pointed elf ears surgically altered so, now, for all intents and purposes, he passed for human. The fact that he was 122 years old had not proved a problem, as yet. He had only been in business for ten years. The time would come when he would have to close his business and start another one under a new name, otherwise his employees would begin to wonder why they were approaching retirement age and their boss still looked as though he was in his thirties.

Zazu was ten years younger than her brother – the baby of the family – and she had sailed through life purely on her looks and ability to accessorize. As soon as she had graduated from school, the Chief Elf had recognised her potential as a buyer for the doll department. It was largely through Zazu's keen eye for fashion trends that the wardrobes of Barbie, Sindy and every other "teen doll" on the market were so hip. She was the first to introduce hair extensions and bling-bling jewellery for the dolls. She had pioneered the manufacture of accessories like miniature iPods, cellphones and laptops. She was also responsible for inventing peel-off nail varnish so that little girls could paint their doll's toes and finger nails and, five minutes later, peel them off and re-do them in another colour.

Zazu, despite having very few intellectual capabilities, had risen through the English elf hierarchy until she was on the Board. It was at the monthly Board meetings that Santa Claus had fallen hopelessly in love with the five foot six elf with long blonde hair, startling green eyes, a smile that could stop men in their tracks and a figure most human women would die for.

Their marriage had not been looked on kindly by the Yule Dynasty. Marrying outside of the Dynasty was frowned upon and marrying a tall elf was definitely not approved of. Still Zazu and Santa had defied the critics and proved them wrong. They were still together and still devoted to each other after forty two years. Nick was their only child, as yet, but at least they had one. Many Yule family members had predicted that the marriage of two different races would never produce a healthy child but Nick came along and he was just fine. He didn't even have elfin ears.

Zazu adored her son and husband and she didn't mind a bit that they had gone to the Yule conference without her. They had discussed going as a family but Santa did not want his wife to be ignored or excluded by the other wives and she didn't want her son to be embarrassed.

Now there was this Christmas Emergency and Zazu felt proud that she would be able to help, although her husband had been very insistent, when he phoned her, that Egan should be there to supervise everything. So, Egan had come up from the South, and brother and sister were now standing in a field waiting for the family sleigh to arrive.

It was, therefore, something of a surprise when a sleek red

Ferrari came hurtling out of the night sky and settled noiselessly on the wet grass.

"Superb!" Egan murmured appreciatively and Zazu teetered across the field to smother her only son with kisses.

"Sweet pea, sugar plum, button!" she squealed, using all the fond names guaranteed to humiliate a teenage boy.

"Mum, mum…" Nick struggled in vain to disengage his mother. Egan winked at him.

Christine and Little K stepped out and grinned.

"Mum!" Nick finally prised Zazu free. "These are my friends, Christine and Little K. Guys, this is my mum, Zazu, and my uncle Egan."

"Pleased to meet you." Christine extended her hand and Egan shook it warmly. She had never seen a tall elf before and she thought he was very handsome. His blonde hair casually flopped over his emerald green eyes and he gave Christine a dazzling smile. She blushed furiously.

Little K bowed and Egan returned the bow.

"Oh so cute!" Zazu's voice had risen to a delighted squeak and she hobbled around the car to hug her son's friends.

"Zazu, you *have* to change your shoes before we leave." Egan was firm. "Let's go to the house, get our luggage and then be on our way. Come on, I'll give you a piggy back."

Christine smiled as they all traipsed through the field to the large house beyond. Egan carried Zazu in a piggy back while she happily prattled on to Christine about how she was "*just* the right size" and she would sort out some of her designer clothes that she "*never* wore" and Christine would look "absolutely *adorable*."

"I forgot to mention that my mum is a bit flaky," Nick whispered in Christine's ear.

"I think she's wonderful. So beautiful," Christine whispered back, "and I think your uncle is very handsome."

Nick gave Christine a puzzled, slightly scornful look, which she ignored.

The Claus house was big and old, like one of those English mansions Christine had seen in movies. The staircase was massive and the fireplace in the living room held a crackling fire made up of, at least, half a big tree.

"Egan, give the boys a snack while I get changed," said Zazu airily. "Christine, you come with me and help me choose some earrings." She linked arms with Christine, as though they were school friends, and propelled her towards the big staircase.

Egan looked thoughtfully at the two boys. "Ham and eggs?" he enquired.

"Do we have time to cook something?" Nick asked.

"Don't be silly, your mother could be at least an hour choosing a pair of earrings."

Nick accepted the truth of this and the three of them ambled off to the kitchen.

Upstairs, Zazu threw open a door. "My dressing room," she said brightly. "I'm almost packed."

Christine stared in open-mouthed astonishment. The room had to be twenty feet square and it was lined with clothes along all three walls. Above the rails were shelves containing hat boxes, boxes of gloves and handbags. Below the rails were shelves filled with more shoes than Christine had ever seen in her life.

"See if you can find me a pair of sensible shoes, sweetheart." Zazu said the word "sensible" with a shudder and Christine began to scan the rows of strappy, jewelled, flower-strewn, embroidered footwear. So far, there was not a flat sole in sight, nor a hint of rubber or plain leather. Zazu, meanwhile, was standing on a little step-stool, in order to lift down one of her many jewellery boxes.

"I have to find a pair of earrings which match my lavender jacket. I'll just take these into the bedroom and tip them on the bed."

Christine found a pair of black ankle boots with a fairly low heel and she took them in the bedroom to show Zazu.

"What do you think, sweet pea?" Zazu held up an earring to her ear and draped the lavender jacket over her shoulder.

"Great," said Christine, trying to be helpful.

"I'm not sure. I think this jacket needs something that dangles more." She noticed the boots in Christine's hand. "Oh, you've found something! I'd forgotten about these. Just perfect!"

She turned her attention to the mound of glittering jewellery on the bed. Other earrings were tried and discarded, then Zazu said,

"Sugar plum, there's a large trunk on the corner of my dressing room. It's filled with clothes that I just don't want anymore. Go and scrabble around and see if you like any of them."

Christine obeyed and soon, they were at opposite mirrors – Christine on one side of the room, trying on clothes and Zazu on the other side, trying and re-trying earrings.

Downstairs, the men folk had finished their ham and eggs and Nick was contentedly wiping a piece of bread around some egginess on his plate.

"Better now?" Egan asked. He knew that his nephew hated sweet Christmassy food and probably found the Yule conference menus a bit of a trial. Nick nodded happily.

Throughout the meal, Egan had quizzed Little K about his magical Christmas lights. He had been impressed and, with his razor-sharp business brain working on overdrive, had privately decided that he was going to draw up a distribution agreement to make himself the sole UK agent for these lights. He could see their potential, even if the Yule Dynasty couldn't. Maybe he could even wangle the European rights before any of the French or Italian Yules came to their senses.

Christine and Zazu appeared, struggling with three large suitcases. Egan groaned.

"Zazu, This job is only going to take a couple of days! What on earth do you need all those clothes for?"

Zazu smiled sweetly. "Only one of the cases is mine, brother dear. The other two are filled with clothes I'm giving to Christine."

Christine was ecstatic. Much as she loved Ma Kringle - and

there was no better mother in the world - Ma's idea of clothes shopping was, well, practical, to say the least. Black shoes, white socks, white underwear - Ma said you could never have too many pairs of white knickers - white blouses, red skirts and so on. For the last half hour, Christine had been in a frenzy of sequins, flower prints, chiffon and lace. She felt drunk with girliness. Zazu had added a whole load of unwanted jewellery as well. Christine hoped that she would not grow out of the clothes too quickly. She looked at Zazu's slim body and prayed that the Yule genes would not kick in for a while. Ma was decidedly ample and they did say that if you wanted to know what a girl would look like in middle age, you only had to look at her mother.

Everyone made their way to the Ferrari, gleaming quietly in the middle of the field in the glow from the house lights.

Egan was pushing a trolley piled up with several cardboard boxes. They contained a new product he was anxious to try out on the public.

"Just chocolates," he said airily when Nick asked him what they were. "You never know when you might need a box of chocolates."

"Will we get everything in the trunk?" Zazu asked.

"Of course, Mum, look!" Nick opened up and they all peered in at the vast space.

"Babbo Natale had car specially designed to accommodate toys for all the children of Italy" explained the scientific Japanese boy. He began to talk about the physics of a huge space being inside a smaller space but trailed off as he realised no-one would be able to understand it. "Magic..." he said instead and everyone went, "Oh!" and smiled.

Bags were loaded and Egan snuck a quick look at the magic lights, writhing fitfully under their covers.

"Be careful!" Little K warned. "If they get out they will decorate the whole field!"

Egan shook his head in wonderment, the details of his agency agreement already forming in his head.

The space inside the passenger part of the car was *not* magic and they all squashed themselves in as best as they could – Zazu, Christine and Little K in the back, Nick in the driving seat and Egan beside him.

"Set a course south-southwest for Plinkbury," said Little K, scanning his calculations under the car's interior light.

"Righto. Fasten your seat belts." Nick went through the procedures for lift off and the Ferrari taxied slowly down the field.

"Lift off!" Nick announced, flipping the gears into F and everyone was thrown back into their seats.

"Plinkbury next stop!"

"They have no idea what's about to hit them!" said Christine delightedly, as, once more, the car took to the skies.

CHAPTER TEN

Drizzle and Depression

Three men and an elf stared at the empty space in the transport hangar where Babbo Natale's Ferrari should have been.

Babbo Natale had a splitting headache. He had spent the whole day defending himself against, what he called "the radical forces in the Yule Dynasty", in other words, The Sisterhood. He had hoped to come down and unburden himself to his beloved Rosa – that was what he called his car. It was named after his wife, Mama Rosa, but that was just for protection. His wife had told him once that he talked in his sleep. So he figured that if he talked about his car in his sleep, his wife would think that he was dreaming about her.

The wife couldn't have been more different from the car. Mama Rosa nagged, Rosa the Ferrari purred. Mama Rosa never listened to her husband, Rosa the car just sat quietly whilst her master poured out his troubles. He liked to think that she (he always thought of his car as female) sat in quiet sympathy while he moaned and complained. He found comfort in his car and now, when he needed her most, she was gone.

Kriss Kringle and Santa of England had come down to the transport hangar to move the American sleigh over a little, so that the gap left by the English sleigh would not be apparent. But they had found the sleigh exactly where it should be…and a large empty space where the Ferrari should have been. Pa Kringle tried to tell himself that the children hadn't left yet but he knew, when he listened to the slightly drunk and nervously sweating Guido, that the Ferrari was now in England and, if it didn't come back in one piece, they were all going to be in terrible trouble.

Guido was mumbling something about the car being taken away for a special free wash and wax job. It would take a couple of days but the car would come back even better than before – honest.

The three men looked doubtfully at the elf. Babbo Natale's head hurt too much to try and figure out what was going on. His eyes narrowed. Tomorrow, when he felt better, he would get the truth out of Guido. He also suspected that his American and English cousins had something to do with it. They looked guilty to him but, maybe, he was just being paranoid. After a day of persecution at the hands of The Sisterhood, anyone would feel paranoid. He decided to take two aspirin and go to bed. Perhaps the car would be back in the morning. He turned on his heel and left.

The person who *was* seeing the bright red Ferrari, at that very moment, thought he was hallucinating. Sergeant George Hill of the Worcestershire County Police was sitting, half-dozing in the centre of Plinkbury town square when he *thought* he saw a red sports car fly past the gothic towers of the Town Hall and descend towards the outer edge of the town. He reasoned to himself that he was tired. It wasn't possible to see a flying car. Well, maybe it was. Maybe it was some child's remote control car that he was playing with in the garden – in the dark – and it just happened to fly up in the air. Yes. That was it. A toy. Or something. Whatever it was, he wasn't going to mention it to anyone. He was one week away from retirement and he did not want to go down in police history as being the first uniformed officer to see a UFO shaped like a Ferrari. It was probably something to do with all those wretched media people who were now camped out, in and around Plinkbury, waiting for a story to break. Perhaps they were trying to create a story. Well he wasn't going to be the patsy who stood in front of the cameras and said that he had seen a flying car. No sir. No way. He took a swig of his, by now, cold coffee and struggled to stay awake.

The Ferrari glided smoothly down into a very quiet suburban

road and glided slowly along the centre as though it were an airport runway.

"It's number 47," said Zazu from the back of the car. "The bed and breakfast place. Mrs Holland at number 47 Valley Drive."

Egan counted out the house numbers and Nick brought the car to a standstill at the kerb outside number 47.

"It doesn't look very luxurious." Egan liked his comfort.

"It was the best I could do!" Zazu was aggrieved. "Everywhere is full! Taken by tv and radio crews and newspaper journalists, apparently."

"Mmm. The fact that this place was *turned down* by everyone else speaks volumes," Egan responded drily, resigning himself to a couple of nights of hard beds and bad food.

Everyone decamped from the Ferrari and unloaded the basic necessities of their luggage. Except Zazu, who said she absolutely needed a suitcase, a vanity case and a jewellery case. Rain was drizzling down in a fine mist and, before they had taken the ten steps from the car to the house, they were all cold and wet.

The door was opened by the most depressed woman anyone had ever seen. She had grey hair scraped back into a net, spectacles so thick that they made her watery blue eyes look enormous and she was wearing black crimplene trousers and a stained Aran sweater. The whole effect was sad and lumpy. Zazu emitted a gasp of pity, as though she had just seen a starving stray dog.

"Mrs Holland?" Egan enquired with practised charm.

"You must be the Christmas family," she said, looking at them with suspicion in her magnified eyes. "Are you journalists?" she injected a fair amount of venom into the question.

"Certainly not!" Zazu was affronted.

"Not at all," said Egan with amusement. "Have you had a lot of trouble with them then?"

"They've been around asking stupid questions. I just slam the door in their face. I've told one or two of them that I don't have any feelings about Christmas, one way or the other. I don't celebrate it and I couldn't care less whether other people do or not."

There was a collective intake of breath from everyone on the doorstep. Christine wondered if all the people in Plinkbury hated Christmas. No wonder the Council had been able to ban it so easily.

Mrs Holland had still not invited them in. In fact it was beginning to look as though they might not have a bed for the night at all and Nick's teeth were beginning to chatter, he was so cold.

"Is Christmas your real name?" Mrs Holland was looking suspiciously at them again.

Egan decided he would have to work the full force of his charm on this woman, if they were to stand any chance of getting in out of the cold.

"Yes, I'm afraid it is," he said brightly. "It's been the curse of our lives, up until now. It's because our family name is Christmas, that we have been invited to Plinkbury by the television companies. They want to do a piece on us. You know – a jokey piece – about how the council can't ban *everything* to do with Christmas because they can't force us to change our names!" He laughed hollowly and Mrs Holland raised one eyebrow.

"Mmph. Well you'd better come in, I suppose." She grudgingly moved away from the door and allowed them to enter.

"You're wet," she said, setting her mouth in a grim line. "Make sure you wipe your feet and take off your shoes. I don't want muddy footprints in my hall."

Everyone looked around at the sad hallway. The wallpaper looked as faded as Mrs Holland and the carpet was practically threadbare. Christine wondered how anyone with such a dilapidated house could have the cheek to object to muddy footprints.

"Let me introduce everyone…" Egan started to say, but Mrs Holland silenced him with a wave of her hand.

"It's not necessary," she said bluntly. "Just pay the room rate in advance and turn up promptly at 8.30 for breakfast." She shuffled ahead of them. Christine noticed that she was wearing very battered old carpet slippers. Zazu had noticed them as well and her lips trembled. How could anyone put such vile objects on their feet?

"This is the breakfast room," she said, opening a door and displaying a fairly spartan room with one large table, six dining chairs and a serving hatch in the wall into the kitchen. "Now I'll take you up to your rooms. Follow me."

They filed up the stairs behind her. Nick noted that the house felt just as cold as the street outside.

"This is the room for you and the two boys," she said, looking at Egan.

They all peered in the room. There were two single beds, covered in blue worn-out candlewick bedspreads, one camp bed, one ancient wardrobe and one battered table lamp.

"And this is the room for the woman and the girl." She spoke about Christine and Zazu as if they weren't there. The room now on display was very much like the other one, except the bedspreads were faded pink. Even the sheets and pillowcases were pink, so Christine began to feel that there was a little ray of hope as far as Mrs Holland was concerned. Perhaps they could introduce the spirit of Christmas into her life, as well as the lives of the other residents of Plinkbury?

"This is the bathroom," Mrs Holland said as she opened a door next to the 'girl's room'. "You'll have to share."

"Fine," said Egan, ignoring Zazu's little squeak of dismay.

"That will be ninety pounds in advance, for the two rooms for three nights."

Egan produced his wallet and began to count out the money.

"No visitors, food or alcohol in your rooms. No noise after ten p.m. No baths or showers after nine p.m. Breakfast, as I said, is at eight thirty a.m. sharp. And you have to be out of your rooms by ten in the morning and not return until five in the evening. I don't do any other meals, so you'll have to eat lunch and dinner out. I don't give any of my guests a key. You have to be back in the house by nine thirty each evening or the front door is locked. Understood?"

They all nodded bleakly and Mrs Holland shuffled off down the stairs, without a smile or a backward glance.

Everyone looked at each other.

"Now we know why this was the only place available," Nick whispered to his mother.

"What could I do? We had to have somewhere to sleep!" she hissed back at him.

"Let's get unpacked and go and have a look at the town," was Egan's whispered suggestion.

"Why are we all whispering?" Christine asked in a normal voice and made them all jump.

"Never mind. Let's just get into some dry clothes and get out of here," said Nick crossly. He could feel one of his headaches coming on.

Within half an hour they were dry and dressed in warm clothes and waterproofs and on their way out of the door.

"We're going out for a meal Mrs Holland!" called Egan towards the half-open living room door, where they could see their landlady slumped in front of the television.

She grunted but her eyes never left the screen. "Door's locked at 9.30," she reminded them as they stepped out into the street.

"Poor woman," said Zazu, her kindness coming to the fore. "I have to take her in hand." Everyone looked at her, quizzically.

"I mean, anyone who wears clothes like that is obviously a very sad person," she answered, by way of explanation. "I can't ignore a cry for help."

They strolled casually into the centre of town. It had stopped raining but the night was becoming cold and clear and the wet streets were rapidly turning to ice. Zazu, as usual, was wearing unsuitable shoes and she clung on to her brother as her stilettos began to slip on the icy ground.

Plinkbury was very small and the town square was nothing to look at. It was dominated by the grandeur of the Town Hall, which stood at the north side of the square. A relic of the Victorian era, it stood dark and forbidding with its stone pillars and wrought iron balconies.

Around the square were some small shops. A newsagents; a jewellers; a shoe shop (displaying the sort of shoes that caused Zazu to make a small noise of disgust); a school outfitters; a real estate agency and a bakery. Two of the shops were empty. In the centre of the square was a small garden, with two benches and some indifferent flower beds. All in all, Plinkbury presented a dismal picture of neglect. If there had ever been any life in the town, it had long since been sucked out. Christine could imagine that it would be quite a jolly place if it were decorated for Christmas and if, perhaps, it had a little street market in the garden. It was as if the Town Council's decision to ban Christmas had been the last nail in Plinkbury's coffin. Tomorrow, on the first day of December, the town would be buried forever.

It was now seven in the evening and the town was *closed*. Except, there were some sounds of life coming from behind the Town Hall. They followed the sounds, turned the corner and found themselves looking at the one pub in Plinkbury that was open – and it was bursting at the seams.

Every newspaper, radio and television journalist, sound crew and camera crew that had been sent to this forgotten part of England, was in the pub, because there was nowhere else to go. It was like a small part of London had been transplanted there and, as far as the landlord of the pub was concerned, it was the best thing that had ever happened to him.

Egan pushed his way to the bar, leaving the others congregated in a huddle inside the door.

"Do you have a table where my family can have a meal?!" Egan bawled at the barman, over the noise.

The barman smiled and shook his head, unable to make himself heard. He just waved his arms at the human throng, by way of explanation. Egan struggled back to the others.

"There's nowhere to sit!" he shouted at them. "We'll never get served here!"

Everyone looked disappointed, except Zazu, who made an impatient "tut!" at her brother's lack of initiative.

"Just wait a minute!" she yelled and she took off her woolly hat and let her long blonde hair fall down to her waist. Then she removed her waterproof coat and handed it to Nick. Underneath she was wearing a very tight dress, low-cut and very short, which left nothing to the imagination. The pub went silent, except for the voices of a few female journalists who were talking in one corner. A vast sea of men eyed Zazu appreciatively. Egan chortled and Nick blushed. Sometimes his mother could be so embarrassing.

Zazu sashayed over to the nearest table and smiled. Mens' mouths fell open. She bent over to speak to them and all the men, who were standing, craned their necks to look at her rear view. Something like a tiny sigh of wishful thinking rippled around the crowd.

"Have you boys finished eating?" she asked softly and the men with the open mouths nodded like imbeciles. "Then do you think that my family could sit here and have a meal?"

The men stood up, as one, and backed away from the chairs. Christine, Nick and Little K made a graceless dash for the seats, before the spell was broken. Egan casually took a seat and said "thank you," and the men seemed to recover their senses, murmuring an awkward "O.K" and "Don't mention it," as they retreated into the crowd.

Zazu perched herself on the remaining seat with a smug look on her face.

The noise in the pub slowly crept back up, though not to its previous ear-splitting level. Christine judged that too many of the men were lost in their own thoughts as they continued to stare at Zazu.

"I'll order some food," said Egan briskly and turned everyone's attention to the menu.

Watching Zazu eat was the highlight, so far, of the media's stay in Plinkbury. Every newspaper, radio station and tv station had rushed some representatives to the town, expecting that the ban on Christmas would provide them with a parcel of stories that would last right through the festive season. But they had not realised just how apathetic the townspeople were. Twenty years of being ignored, bypassed, bad Council decisions and declining employment had taken its toll. People only lived in Plinkbury because it was cheap. Everyone commuted to other towns to work. By day the town was almost as dead as it was by night. There was no cinema, no restaurants, only one pub that opened in the evenings and precious little to do. The journalists and reporters were bored out of their minds and, if nothing happened tomorrow, most of them were going to abandon Plinkbury to its fate and go and find some real stories.

Egan had analysed the problem in a few short minutes. His mind had been working overtime since he had surveyed, tonight, the depths to which the town had sunk. They were here to save Christmas in Plinkbury but Egan had plans that would last far beyond the festive season. He smiled to himself as his thoughts formed, like a jigsaw, into a beautiful picture.

Some twenty five miles away from Plinkbury, in the town of Nether-Pilsbury, Egan's best customer, Mrs Bella Shuttleworth, could hardly sleep for excitement. Her husband eyed her wearily. Yesterday, she had received a new catalogue from The Christmas Shop and a special letter. The letter had read:

Valued Customer,

You may be aware that the town of Plinkbury has banned Christmas. As a lover of all Christmas things yourself, you will probably feel, as I do, that this is a shameful situation. Therefore, I am asking all regular customers of the Christmas Shop catalogue, who live within striking distance of Plinkbury, to join me in Plinkbury Town Square to protest about this disgraceful council decision. All those who attend, to take part in the demonstration, will receive a special edition American Holiday Dinner Service – four place settings – as a thank you gift. Please gather in Plinkbury Town Square at 12 noon on the 1st December. Santa hats are optional. Refreshments will be provided.

Yours sincerely,

Egan

Managing Director of The Christmas Shop and The Festive Import/Export Company.

Bella Shuttleworth had been beside herself. An American Holiday Dinner Service! Only the most sought after Christmas merchandise in the history of Christmas memorabilia!

Bella was an avid collector. All of Egan's mail order customers were Christmas nuts. They lived and breathed Christmas. They scoured the world for Christmas mugs; china figures; handmade decorations; cushion covers – anything to do with Christmas was their lifelong obsession.

The Shuttleworth house looked perfectly normal from the outside. Standard semi-detached. Roses growing around the door.

Neatly manicured lawn. But, inside, it was like a demented Santa's Grotto. Every square inch of the walls in the hallway, living room and dining room, were covered in plates depicting Christmas scenes and figures. Every surface – sideboard, shelves, mantelpiece – were covered with little snow-covered houses; china Christmas trees; china elves; Santas and fairies. Their red sofa and chairs were littered with Christmas cushions. The tea towels were Christmassy; the rugs were Christmassy, the curtains were made of red fabric with holly sprigs; the vases contained artificial Christmas roses, holly and poinsettias. And it was like that all year round.

Mr Shuttleworth tolerated his wife's obsessive hobby because, when Christmas actually came around, he could indulge in his obsession with Christmas lights. Each year he would set up as many lights and animated figures as he could physically load onto the house and into the garden. People drove for thirty miles to come and see the Shuttleworth Christmas lights. They would step out of their cars, put on their sunglasses and stare in amazement. Last year, Harold Shuttleworth raised £4,732.09 for the local hospice and this year he was going to improve on that.

The Shuttleworths lay side by side in their massive bed, covered in its Christmas patchwork bedspread, with their heads resting on pillowcases embroidered with holly sprigs.

"How many people are coming tomorrow?" Harold asked nervously.

"All the members of The Christmas Convention," Bella said excitedly. The Christmas Convention was a local club Bella had set up fifteen years ago for all lovers of Christmas merchandise. "All twenty three of them," she added. "And the local branch of the Women's Institute decided that they would come along as well. So that's another nineteen."

"Are they all going in their own cars?" asked her incredulous husband.

"No. Mabel Allardyce has persuaded her husband to provide a bus for the day."

All of this had been arranged in the last twenty four hours. The moment Egan's catalogues had plopped on to the doormats of his Valued Customers, the obsessive Christmas collectors had swung into action. Egan knew his customers so well. As soon as the news about Plinkbury had broken, Egan's staff had sent out the special mail shot guaranteed to mobilise a sizeable army of Christmas fanatics. Of course, it was going to cost him money. Giving away American Holiday Dinner Services would not be cheap but it would be worth it in terms of good publicity for his business.

As Bella Shuttleworth was trying to get to sleep, Egan and the others were also trying to get to sleep in Mrs Holland's unpleasant establishment.

The beds were hard and creaky. The rooms were cold and depressing. Egan fastidiously decided he would sleep on top of the eiderdown, as the sheets looked suspiciously grubby, and he was lying, fully clothed, covered by his sister's marabou trimmed, velvet dressing gown. The two teenage boys, not at all bothered about the state of the sheets, were sleeping peacefully after a long and eventful day.

In the 'girl's room', Zazu, who rarely went to sleep before midnight, was engaged in her lengthy beauty routine, much to Christine's fascination. First the make-up came off (and Christine noted that Zazu was just as beautiful without make-up and she looked startlingly young), then the various cleansing, massaging, toning and nourishing of the face, neck, arms, shoulders and legs began.

Zazu prattled on about everything that was going to happen tomorrow.

"...so, I've persuaded Egan to let me stay here in the morning, while the rest of you go and do your things," she said, opening pot number five and applying its contents to her elbows.

"But Mrs Holland won't let anyone stay in the house during the day," Christine sleepily pointed out.

"Don't you worry about that." Zazu gave an enigmatic smile as she proceeded to brush her long blonde hair for the required one hundred strokes. "By lunchtime, I shall have transformed that woman." It was a statement of fact, not hope. Zazu seemed so confident, that Christine wished that she could stay behind in the morning as well, so that she could see this promised miracle. But there was far too much to be done. They had a deadline to meet. She smiled as Zazu finished her beauty routine by spraying a mist of perfume in the air and walking through it.

"Sleep well, angel face," Zazu murmured and kissed Christine on the forehead before she put out the light. Christine drifted off in a cloud of fragrance into the deepest sleep she had ever known.

By contrast, in the Arctic north, Pa Kringle was still pacing the floor, unable to sleep at all.

"How could you let them take that valuable car?!" This was the fifteenth time Pa had asked Ma the same question and she was beginning to get a little tired of it all.

"For the last time, Pa, the kids decided, quite rightly, that they would have nowhere to hide a sleigh. They couldn't leave it parked outside in the road. But they could leave a car parked outside. It was the most sensible thing."

Kriss heard the explanation again but he wasn't really listening. All he could think about was the fact that Babbo Natale was going to get very nasty when he found out. His Italian cousin had always made him a little nervous, since they were small boys. The memories of Young Natale giving him a Chinese burn, or stuffing his head down the toilet, or twisting his arm up his back, still made him shudder. You didn't mess with Babbo Natale – he had a very short fuse.

Still, he reasoned, perhaps he wouldn't find out. Perhaps they could all keep up the pretence that the car had gone for a wash and wax job. But, in his heart of hearts, he knew that the elf, Guido, was about to crack and reveal everything. But, then, what did Guido know? According to Ma, the elf genuinely believed that the car was being cleaned. That's what the kids had told him and that's all he could tell his boss. The fact that the kids were missing had not been noticed by anyone. How long before it was? There were just too many questions buzzing around in his head to allow him to sleep, so he sat down and had another cup of hot chocolate with cinnamon, to calm his nerves. Despite his anxiety, he did eventually fall asleep – sitting up, in a chair, head sunk on his chest, muttering to himself, "If you touch me again, I'll tell my dad," as he dreamt about Babbo Natale giving him another Chinese burn.

☆

CHAPTER ELEVEN

The Troops Gather

Breakfast, at Mrs Holland's, was to be endured, rather than enjoyed. The room was cold, as were the bowls of grey porridge plonked down in front of everyone. Then the bacon was overcooked, the eggs were undercooked and the mushrooms appeared to be swimming in a little pool of grease. Everyone helped themselves liberally to bread and butter and fought away the nausea.

It didn't bother Zazu too much. She hardly ever ate breakfast. The coffee, at least, was drinkable.

"Is there a Mr. Holland?" she enquired casually as the landlady put a plate of cold, rubbery toast on the table.

The question drew a glare from Mrs Holland. "There is a Mr Holland *somewhere*," she said between gritted teeth. "He'd just better not show his face around here, that's all. He ran off with another woman and good riddance."

"Oh I am sorry." Zazu didn't sound sorry. In fact she sounded rather triumphant. She had suspected something of the sort had happened to this unfortunate woman and now she knew exactly which buttons to press to unlock Mrs Holland's hidden potential.

Upstairs, they all gathered and synchronised watches.

"Right," said Egan briskly. "We all know what we're doing. Nick and Christine, have you got notebooks and pencils?" Both of them nodded and held them up. "Little K, have you got a sketchpad and pencil?" He nodded too and held them up.

"Zazu," said Egan, turning his attention to his sister, "you have to be in the town square at noon. It's absolutely vital. Understand?"

Zazu raised an eyebrow.

"Have you got the costume?" Egan continued, "Have you got the car keys and are you sure you know how to drive it?"

"For goodness sake, Egan!" Zazu hated it when her brother bossed her around. "I'm only going to drive it to the Town Square. I'm not going to fly it or anything!"

Egan looked steadily at Zazu. Against his better judgement, he decided to trust her. "Ok, let's get this show on the road," he said, with the determination of a general at the head of his troops.

In the town square of Plinkbury, the shopkeepers were just opening up. Mr Patel, the newsagent, waved politely to Mr Rosenbaum, the jeweller, across the square. Mr Rosenbaum returned the wave.

"How's business?" Mr Rosenbaum always called out.

"Not very good." Mr Patel always replied.

Come rain or shine, summer or winter, that's all that the two men ever said to each other, apart from, at the end of each day,

"Another day over."

"Let's hope tomorrow's better."

Plinkbury had that effect on people. There was a kind of submission which settled over everybody when they had lived there for a few months.

When Mr Patel had first moved into the town, he had been full of enthusiasm. His little shop had been filled with sweets and knick-knacks, he had even tried to stock knitting wool and DVDs but, gradually, he came to realise that his customers were simply not interested. His business kept ticking over because everyone who worked in the Town Hall stopped in his shop to buy their newspapers and their packets of mints or barley sugar. No-one ever stopped for a chat or gave him a smile – except at Christmas. As soon as he decorated his shop each year, the customer's moods seemed to lighten. For the whole month of December, they would behave like human beings and engage in conversations. Now, even that had been taken away by the killjoys on the Council and he didn't have the heart to protest.

As he set out his newspaper headline placard, he noticed some new people walking around the square. A good-looking man and three children. He sighed. Probably something to do with TV or radio, he thought, and he went back inside his shop.

Egan marshalled the gang in the square.

"Right. Chris and Nick, you start the interviews. K, you start making your calculations. I have to go to the pub and then the real estate agents. We'll meet back here in half an hour."

Everyone dispersed. Little K sat down on one of the benches in the central garden and stared thoughtfully at the Town Hall. His task was to calculate how many strings of lights they should throw at the building. He began to count the balconies and pillars and scribble on his pad.

Christine and Nick walked along one side of the square. Their task was to talk to the shopkeepers. They stopped outside Mr Patel's shop.

"This looks a good bet," Christine whispered. "Look, proprietor S.Patel. Ready?"

"Ready." Nick sounded confident, so they stepped into the shop.

Mr Patel looked up gloomily from his newspaper. The children he had seen earlier were browsing around the shelves. "Can I help you?" he asked them politely.

"Actually, you can," said Nick, smiling at the shopkeeper. "We're doing a piece for our school newspaper about the ban on Christmas and we wondered if you would mind answering a few questions?"

Mr Patel shrugged. There was nothing else to do, so why not?

Nick looked at his pad. "I hope you don't think I'm being rude but I take it, from your name, that you are not a Christian?"

Mr Patel frowned. "No, Hindu." He wasn't sure about the

direction that this questioning was going to take, so he wasn't prepared to be friendly just yet.

At that moment, two customers came into the shop. A man and a woman. They were both Council employees, from the Town Hall, about to start the working day.

"The Daily Herald, please," said the man. Mr Patel duly obliged.

"A packet of mints, please," said the woman, as she handed over the money.

Neither of the customers smiled. Mr Patel called after them, as they walked towards the door.

"Don't forget to buy an advent calendar! It's nearly December!"

The customers turned and looked at him blankly.

"What for?" asked the man.

"Advent calendars are for children and I don't have any," said the woman.

They both left and a depressed Mr Patel turned back to Nick.

Nick smiled again. Mr Patel was watching Christine, who was looking at some Christmas cards. He wasn't sure whether this was just some clever diversionary tactic. Perhaps the boy was going to distract him while the girl stole something. He cleared his throat.

"Is she with you?" he asked Nick, suspiciously.

Nick nodded. "Oh yes. Christine come over here, you're making Mr Patel nervous." Nick realised that Mr Patel was unsure about them.

Christine hastily joined Nick. "Sorry," she said. "I was just admiring your Christmas stuff."

"Huh!" Mr Patel's voice took on a sarcastic edge. "You're the only one who is. Come back next week and I'll be selling everything at half price. No-one is buying it."

"Ah," Nick sounded sympathetic. "So this ban on Christmas has affected your trade then?"

"I should say it has!" Mr Patel's voice rose a little in exasperation. He moved out from behind his counter and strode down the aisles. "You see all this stuff?" He pointed towards all the Christmas cards and paper. "I should be starting to order in extra stock by now! First of December today. I usually decorate the shop in the last week of November and everyone starts buying their Christmas stuff straight away. I haven't sold one Christmas card! Not one!" He sounded bitter.

Nick began to follow him around the shop. "So, as a Hindu, you're not offended by Christmas at all, then?"

Mr Patel straightened up from rearranging some magazines.

"Offended? Why would I be offended? I celebrate Christmas as well as Diwali. In my house we have a Christmas tree. My children get presents. I *like* Christmas! It's the best part of the English winter! My *customers* used to like Christmas! It used to be the only time they would smile at me and say, 'How are you?' Why would anybody think I would be offended by Christmas? Only that pack of lunatics in the Town Hall. They think Christmas offends ethnic minorities. So what do they do? They fix it so that this ethnic minority..." he slapped his chest with his hand in an agitated manner "...this particular ethnic minority is going to go out of business! Lunatics!" He muttered to himself and vigorously rearranged the magazines once more.

"So why don't you protest?" Christine asked.

Mr Patel glared at her. "Are you American?"

"Er, yes. I've just moved over here."

"Well let me tell you, Miss America, if I protest - if I put Christmas decorations up - I will get fined fifty pounds for every day they are up there. Fifty pounds a day! I can't *afford* to protest! Also..." he added bitterly, "if I don't sell all this Christmas stock I shall go out of business anyway. It's a no-win situation."

"That's terrible," Nick said, sympathetically. "May I ask you one last question, please?"

"No. No more questions!" Mr Patel was now in a very bad mood. Talking about his dilemma had made it seem much worse.

Nick persisted. "I was just going to ask - if there was an

organised protest in the town square today, would you join in?"

Mr Patel looked at both of them. "You know something?" he asked hopefully. "There's going to be a protest? Lots of people?"

"Well, we can't say anything definite," answered Christine, lowering her voice conspiratorially, "but we've heard a very strong rumour that something is going to happen today."

Mr Patel's eyes gleamed. "If there is a protest, I might join in. I'll see." He reached behind him and produced two Christmas lollipops. "Here." He offered them to the two friends. "Merry Christmas." Nick and Christine grinned and took the gifts. "Go and see Mr Rosenbaum in the jewellers," Mr Patel added, "ask him what he thinks about Christmas."

Nick and Christine left Mr Patel in a state of excitement. If there were going to be protesters in the square, he was going to get a trestle table out of the back storeroom and put all his best Christmas merchandise on display outside the shop. He wasn't going to put lights up, so they couldn't fine him. Things were looking up.

The two friends stepped into the jeweller's shop. Christine smiled happily at a display of twinkling Christmas earrings. There were little Christmas wreaths and trees, candy canes and gingerbread men. Mr Rosenbaum had artfully placed gold velvet tree-shaped cones around the counters of the shop and all his best jewellery was decorating the cones. The Council had sent an inspector into his shop to complain about the tree-shaped cones because they felt that they looked suspiciously like Christmas decorations. But Mr Rosenbaum had explained that they were standard-issue jewellery display items and not Christmassy at all. The inspector had been forced to withdraw but had threatened to make random inspections throughout December.

Nick launched into his presentation about doing the school newspaper and could he ask a few questions. Mr Rosenbaum was amiable enough, even when Nick asked him if he was a Christian. He shook his head and said he was Jewish.

"Are you offended by Christmas?"

Mr Rosenbaum smiled.

"Not at all," he said. "Christmas is one of the few celebrations that everyone can join in."

"How do you mean?" Christine was curious.

"Well," Mr Rosenbaum explained carefully, "my family celebrates Hanukah *before* Christmas but we rarely ask our Christian friends to celebrate with us because Hanukah is a purely religious celebration. If you are not a member of the Jewish faith you would not understand Hanukah, so we don't share it with non-Jews. Christmas, on the other hand, has evolved into a celebration for everyone. If you are a practising Christian, you can celebrate the religious side of Christmas. If you are not a Christian – even if you are an atheist who doesn't believe in God at all – you can celebrate the secular side of Christmas – the present-giving, the food, and the songs. Most of that part of Christmas is borrowed from the old pagan religions anyway. It's really the festival of Yule, not the Christian celebration of Christmas. It's a celebration of light and warmth during the winter, a time for friendship and gifts. My children and grandchildren don't think of Santa Claus as a Christian gift bringer. To them, he brings gifts for *all* children irrespective of race, creed or colour. Isn't that true?"

Nick was furiously scribbling down the wise words of the jeweller while Christine nodded happily and thought about Pa's speech, folded up in her pocket. Surely, most people felt the same way about Christmas?

Most people, perhaps, but not Agnes Holland. Ever since her husband left, some eight years ago, Christmas had become meaningless to her. She had no children or grandchildren. She only had the television and, in recent years, there had been precious little Christmas cheer on the tv to lighten her spirits. No, Christmas was just another day to her.

She stomped up the stairs, unwilling to make her guests' beds but it had to be done. Arthritis was beginning to make itself felt in most of her joints, so she found the business of bed-making a bit of a chore. She decided to do the "girl's" room first. It would probably be tidier. Boys were nasty, messy creatures and she couldn't abide them. Girls were better.

She opened the door and stood, rooted to the spot in shock. The drab, cheerless room had been transformed into a boudoir. An honest-to-goodness perfume and chiffon boudoir. Zazu had draped chiffon scarves over the window and another scarf, with sequins on it, was draped over the light fitting. The room looked soft and pink. One bed was covered in sparkling jewellery and, hanging along the picture rail, were the sort of clothes that every woman dreams about. Evening dresses, covered in shimmering beads; summer dresses bedecked with flowers; embroidered blouses and glistening, sequinned evening bags. Then there were the shoes – lined up along the floor. Gold, with impossibly high heels; some had impossibly thin metallic straps; there were satin pumps; leather courts; sequinned sandals and so much more.

Standing in the middle of it all was the vision that was Zazu. She was dressed from head to foot in a pale lavender trouser suit, and her long blonde hair down her back like a silken curtain.

Agnes Holland opened her mouth to protest but her eye caught a particularly beautiful black caftan, encrusted with gold and sequins around the neck. A great longing welled up inside her. A deep and long-buried need to be beautiful, to feel silk against her skin, instead of thick wool, and to feel creams and perfumes on her body instead of coal tar soap and chest embrocation.

Zazu smiled knowingly, then she opened a box of Egan's special chocolates. They had been invented by the Chief Elf of England and were, to all intents and purposes, ordinary liqueur chocolates. They were called "Christmas Spirit" and the name was a clue to the secret ingredient that would, Egan hoped, make these chocolates highly sought-after. The mellow liquid inside each chocolate contained real Christmas spirit, distilled from the laughter of all the elves in Santa's employment. One bite and you were filled with an indescribable joy. Zazu held the box out to Agnes Holland. "Have a chocolate," she said softly.

Plinkbury town square was beginning to liven up a little. Several television vans had taken up residence on the south side of the square, opposite the Town Hall, in the vain hope that a story might break today. At the very least, some of the journalists decided that they would get a final quote from the Council Leader, emphasising that Christmas was definitely banned in Plinkbury, then head back to their studios. But, there was a bit of a buzz in the air, as word had spread that the man who was with the gorgeous blonde in the pub last night had placed a very large order with the publican for rolls, sandwiches and drinks. There was a feeling that something might be afoot.

Sergeant George Hill of the Worcestershire County Police was back on duty, sitting in his car on the east side of the square. He was supposed to be there in case there was any kind of rioting. The fact that his superiors had sent just one policeman, who was one week short of retirement, meant that they regarded a civil disturbance in Plinkbury as highly unlikely.

Egan appeared in the square and noted, with satisfaction, that Nick and Christine were having some success interviewing the shopkeepers, judging by the smiles on their faces. They were, indeed, being well received. Mr Rosenbaum had given them both a Christmas brooch and, now, Mrs Smith, in the bakery, had answered all their questions and given them a mince pie each. They turned to go into the shoe shop. Egan waved as he turned to go into the real estate agency.

In a lay-by on the A937, twenty miles outside of Plinkbury, Harry Allardyce was loading forty two excited women and some long-suffering husbands on to his best bus. Quite a few of them were wearing Santa hats, some were wearing Christmas tree hats with flashing baubles and one was sporting an angel costume with sparkly wings. They were in extremely high spirits.

As the coach pulled out onto the road, the women burst into a rousing chorus of "Jingle Bells". Then some of the women shrieked excitedly as Harry Allardyce found himself following a large truck which bore the legend, **THE CHRISTMAS SHOP.**

Down in the valley, the outline of the town of Plinkbury could just be seen in the morning gloom. It sat, squat and colourless, amongst the morning mist. A warty frog of a town, that was about to be turned into a prince.

☆

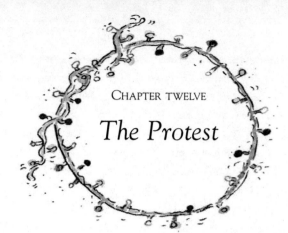

CHAPTER TWELVE

The Protest

Kriss Kringle filed into the conference hall behind the other delegates. He had woken up with a very stiff neck, due to sleeping in a chair all night, and a knot of anxiety in his stomach. Today was the second day of the Emergency Debate, when the Male Gift Bringers got their chance to reply fully to the accusations hurled at them by the The Sisterhood yesterday. He glanced over to Babbo Natale. The Italian was wearing dark glasses this morning and obviously feeling a little fragile.

The atmosphere in the hall was subdued but with an underlying current of anger. The problem was that not all the Male Gift Bringers were in opposition to The Sisterhood. Some of them, particularly the ones who were still firmly allied with the Christian Church – like all the Kings and St.Mikulas and the other Saints – agreed with some of the opinions that were put forward by the Female Gift Bringers. They felt that Christmas had become too commercialised and that the toy manufacturers were taking over the festive season. This lack of solidarity amongst the men was bound to explode into some fairly unpleasant arguments and The Sisterhood would be ecstatic. Kriss Kringle noted, grimly, that the Black Gang were placing themselves strategically around the hall and that they were all carrying the tools of their job – birch switches. Black Peter took his job as Head of Security very seriously indeed.

Kriss had been to some lively Yule conferences in his time but it had never been this bad. What would the general public think if they knew that the Santas of the world were squabbling amongst themselves? Still, while all this was going on, no-one had given any thought to what was happening at Plinkbury. The more time the kids had to remedy the situation, without any interference from the Yule Dynasty, the better it would be. He sighed and took his seat, popping another indigestion tablet in his mouth and reading his speech again, for the umpteenth time.

In Plinkbury, it was now 11.30 a.m. and the media crews were getting a little restless. Several of them had asked to speak to Angela Summer, the Leader of the Council, but she had flatly refused to make herself available. The shopkeepers were behaving oddly too. They were refusing to be interviewed until later. Why? There was an air of expectancy in the town square but no-one knew why.

Suddenly, there was some action. A large truck pulled into one side of the square and was forced to double park, because a BBC Outside Broadcast van was occupying the kerb, and a large bus pulled into the other side of the square, swung round in front of the Town Hall and began to unload excited middle-aged ladies wearing Santa hats. The media crews galvanised into action and began filming. Reporters hovered, unsure which way to turn next.

Egan, a signed lease for one of the empty shops in Plinkbury town square in his pocket, stepped off the pavement to speak to the driver of the truck. He pointed at the empty shop in question and the driver climbed down and opened up the back of the vehicle to reveal Christmas, with a capital C. There were decorated Christmas trees; five foot high, exquisitely dressed Santa figurines, giant snowmen – so many beautiful things – and crates and crates of Christmas merchandise. Egan had decided to open up a new branch of The Christmas Shop, right in front of the Town Hall that had banned Christmas.

After he had issued instructions to the men, he turned his attention to his Valued Customers, who were now milling about on the pavement in front of the Town Hall. Bella Shuttleworth, as the unofficial leader and organiser of the day trip, pushed herself forward to great him.

"Mr Egan?" she enquired breathlessly. "I'm Bella Shuttleworth."

Egan gave her a devastating smile, took her proffered hand and kissed it. Bella Shuttleworth had spent £3,792.17 last year on products from The Christmas Shop catalogue. Egan valued her very highly indeed.

"Bella," he said, gazing deep into her eyes, "I knew I could count on you to support me today."

Bella felt as though she had died and gone to heaven. Not only had she had her hand kissed by the man she had admired from afar for so many years, but he was also the most handsome man she had ever seen. Who said that hobbies can't fill your whole life with joy?

"Ladies! Ladies!" Her voice rose to an emotional shriek. There was silence. "Ladies – oh, and gentlemen, of course – this is Mr Egan, the owner of The Christmas Shop."

There was a spontaneous round of applause and Egan graciously smiled and nodded to all of them.

"I want to thank you all, dear ladies and, of course gentlemen, for rallying to support the cause of Christmas." There were some cheers from the assembled crowd and the television cameras closed in. "The plan is…" Egan continued "that we shall stage our protest here, in front of the Town Hall. In a moment, some banners will be arriving, for you to hold. If any of you need bathroom facilities, the landlord of the pub just around the corner has kindly made them available. He will also be providing you with refreshments today, which will be delivered to the square at lunchtime."

Everyone cheered, then a voice from the back called "Why is The Christmas Shop truck here?" These ladies were nothing if not single-minded. If there was an opportunity to shop, they wanted to know.

"I am, indeed, about to open a branch of The Christmas Shop here in Plinkbury," Egan confirmed. The ladies screamed ecstatically. Several of the accompanying husbands groaned, as they could see that a Worcestershire branch of the shop was going to make a considerable dent in their incomes. "However," Egan continued "The shop will not be open until this evening. As you can see, the stock has just arrived and it will take me the best part of today to get it all in place." There was another round of applause. "There will also be other significant events, later in the day," Egan added, with an enigmatic smile.

The television and radio crews, plus a few late-rising newspaper reporters, began to advance on Egan, clamouring for an interview.

By now, the square was lined with shopkeepers, who had come out of their premises to see what was going on. Nick and Christine were standing outside the school outfitters. Mr Patel was hurriedly putting the final merchandise on the trestle table outside his shop. Police Sergeant George Hill had finally decided to get out of his car and review the situation; members of the Town Council had come out on to the balconies and all the Council employees were looking out the windows.

It was at this moment that the red Ferrari purred into the square, nudged its way through the crowd and glided to the kerb outside the Town Hall. Two women got out of the Ferrari. One was the drop-dead gorgeous blonde that all the media people remembered from the pub. She was wearing the skimpiest of elf costumes. Her long legs were encased in fishnet tights and her feet were shod in little stiletto ankle boots. There was a collective male shudder of appreciation.

The other woman was older, but nonetheless attractive. Her brown hair was swept up into a cascade of curls and she was wearing a cute knee-length Mrs Santa outfit. It was fairly figure-hugging and the older gentlemen in the crowd noted, with satisfaction, that she had very shapely legs and ankles. Sergeant Hill thought that she looked vaguely familiar to him. Nick and Little K wondered aloud who the woman was and Christine laughed.

"It's Mrs Holland!" she said with glee.

The two boys were speechless.

Agnes Holland basked in the admiring glances. She couldn't remember the last time she had felt so glamorous. Up until this point, her life had been so dull, so depressing.

After she had taken the offered chocolate, in the bedroom this morning, it just seemed as though a great, black cloud had lifted from her mind. Life had suddenly been filled with endless possibilities. As though in a dream, she had allowed Zazu to dye her grey hair, pluck her eyebrows and cover her face in a deep-cleansing mask. After two more chocolates, she hadn't even murmured when Zazu waxed her legs. Then the face mask had been taken off, anti-wrinkle cream applied and she had watched in the mirror, astonished, as Zazu expertly styled her hair and applied make-up. The old Agnes Holland had disappeared. Forever. The new Agnes Holland discovered that she had a waist and nice, smooth, shapely legs. The old Agnes Holland had suffered from arthritis and had a bunion developing on the big toe joint of her left foot. The new Agnes Holland had no aches and pains and, as she slid her feet into a stylish pair of black court shoes, with kitten heels, there appeared to be no trace of a bunion. Zazu had painted Agnes' fingernails, sprayed her with perfume, lacquered her hair and then stood back to admire her handiwork.

"Mrs Holland, I do believe that you are gorgeous!"

"I am, aren't I?" Agnes had breathed in wonderment. Then her voice had risen to an excited scream. **"I AM GORGEOUS!"**

It was in that mood of overwhelming gratitude that Agnes had allowed herself to be dressed as "Mrs Santa", while Zazu had put on her sexy elf costume. How they had giggled at the sight of themselves in the mirror! There had just been one moment – one tiny moment – of sadness, when the thought had flitted through Agnes' mind that she had wasted all those years being depressed and burying herself under layers of baggy clothes – but it had passed when Zazu had whispered "Want to go out and show Plinkbury what a doll you are now?"

Did she?! You bet! As she stood in front of the Ferrari, with the television cameras trained on her, she vowed that this would be the beginning of a new life and there would be no going back.

Zazu and Agnes proceeded to unload the banners, which were distributed amongst Bella Shuttleworth's friends and the protest began in earnest.

The protestors moved, in a throng, to the steps of the Town Hall. Someone's husband produced an accordion from a suitcase and a melodic rendering of *Santa Claus is Coming to Town* began.

Zazu and Agnes draped themselves, fetchingly, over the side of the Ferrari, like models at a Motor Show, and the media rushed forward in a frenzy.

By 12.30, the first news items hit the airwaves and the daily papers were taking delivery of colour photos to dominate the front pages of their next-day editions.

Egan had been interviewed by everyone. The publicity for his business was tremendous. He smiled broadly every time a reporter said, "This is Mr Egan, owner of The Christmas Shop, who is defiantly opening a new shop in Plinkbury, the town that banned Christmas."

Zazu and Agnes were interviewed.

"My name is Zazu Christmas and, because of my name, I have always been a lover of everything to do with Christmas." Zazu pouted at the cameras like a true glamour model.

"My name is Agnes Holland and I think everyone should be filled with the spirit of Christmas all year round!" She seemed slightly drunk to most of the reporters, but good value for the camera. Bubbly and attractive middle-aged women were very popular with the viewers. Zazu decided she must tell Egan that the chocolates were a *tiny* bit too strong.

Bella Shuttleworth was interviewed.

"I love Christmas. My house is filled with Christmas all year round and my husband covers our house and garden with five thousand, two hundred and twenty seven lights every December."

The reporters excitedly scribbled down her address in Nether-Pilsbury and made appointments to see the Shuttleworths, at home, the following week, when the lights went up.

Egan wheeled the teenagers forward to be interviewed but the boys were too embarrassed So Christine was interviewed on her own, by Jane Hoffmeyer, the America reporter who had been the first off the mark with the story of the Plinksbury ban.

"So Christine, you are from America, is that right?"

"Yes, I am."

"And why are you involved in this demonstration today?"

Christine took a deep breath and stared briefly up at the bank of microphones suspended above her head. She had spent the last twenty four hours reading and re-reading Pa's speech. She knew most of it by heart, so she spoke calmly and clearly.

"The Council of Plinkbury has a misguided idea that the celebration of Christmas is offensive to ethnic minorities. I come from America, where we have a far bigger melting pot of cultures than you have in England and we feel that, in the 21st century, Christmas unites everyone, of every creed, race and colour, in a winter celebration of love, peace, light and joy. Over the centuries, the day of Christ's birth has become a universal symbol of hope, fellowship and reunion. But other faiths have taken the spirit of Christmas into their hearts without, necessarily, embracing Christianity. The celebration of Christmas has become a good reason for people to stop their hectic lives to give presents and time to family, friends and strangers. No government, national or local, should have the power to take that time of celebration away from the people."

The square erupted into cheers, whistles and applause. When the noise died down, the reporter said solemnly, "It takes a child to tell the adults of the world what Christmas really means. This is Jane Hoffmeyer reporting from the town of Plinkbury in England, where the beaurocrats tried to ban Christmas but the people are fighting back."

It was now lunchtime and the Town Hall employees, always creatures of habit, began to nervously push their way through the protestors to take their lunch breaks.

Zazu took boxes of "Christmas Spirit" chocolates out of the Ferrari and began dispensing them to the shopkeepers. She sweetly recommended that they give their customers a free chocolate with every purchase.

Mr Patel was delighted. Every Town Hall employee was duly handed a free chocolate with their newspaper. He even sampled some himself and very tasty they were too. Mrs Smith, in the bakery, gave a chocolate away with every roll or pie that she sold. The effect of the chocolates had a speedy effect on empty stomachs. Soon, the square was filled with happy council workers, filled with inexplicable joy, linking arms and joining in with the singing from the Town Hall steps.

"*Chestnuts roasting on an open fire..*"

Over a hundred voices rose in unison.

"*Jack Frost nipping at your nose...*"

Zazu winked at Egan.

"*Yuletide carols being sung by a choir...*"

The cameramen were sweating in their efforts to capture all the activity on tape.

"*and folks, dressed up like Eskimos...Everybody knows..*"

Sergeant Hill wondered whether he should call for back up.

"*Some turkey and some mistletoe...*"

Mr Patel had a rush of ecstatic joy and ran into his storeroom to liberate his Christmas lights.

"*Help to make the season bright...*"

Mr Rosenbaum had come out from his shop and was waltzing with Agnes Holland.

"*Tiny tots, with their eyes all aglow.*"

The voices rose to a crescendo,

"*Will find it hard to sleep tonight!*"

The song continued.

"They know that Santa's on his way.."

Mr Patel appeared, carrying a mountain of lights and began to frantically decorate the front of his shop.

"He's loaded lots of toys and goodies on his sleigh..."

Mr Rosenbaum rushed over to help him.

"And every mother's child is gonna spy..."

Mr Patel, with a manic chuckle, inserted the plugs and switched on.

"To see if reindeer really know how to fly.."

The front of Patel's shop burst into a glory of coloured lights and the singers paused briefly to cheer and then resumed.

"And so, I'm offering this simple phrase..."

Two Council inspectors pushed their way through the crowd and advanced on Mr Patel's shop.

"To kids from one to ninety-two.."

Mr Patel reappeared, wearing a Santa hat and eating another chocolate. *"Although it's been said, many times, many ways..."*

He appeared drunk so Sergeant Hill advanced towards him too.

"Me-e-e-rry Christmas to you!"

The crowds burst into joyful pandemonium as the song finished. However, their mood very quickly turned to outrage as they realised that Mr Patel was being arrested.

The camera crews fought to get to the front of the action as the crowd surged forwards from the Town Hall steps and the square.

Mr Patel was shouting "I'm a Hindu and I love Christmas! Down with Plinkbury Council !" as he was unceremoniously shoved into the back of the police car.

"Down with the Council!" The council employees began to chant rhythmically. Everyone else joined in.

"DOWN WITH THE COUNCIL!"
"DOWN WITH THE COUNCIL!"
"DOWN WITH THE COUNCIL!"

Jane Hoffmeyer shouted to her camera.

"As you can see and hear around me, what was a peaceful and

joyful demonstration in the town of Plinkbury, has now turned ugly, as one of the shopkeepers has been arrested for putting up Christmas lights over his shop. The mood of the crowd which. moments ago, was filled with Christmas spirit, has now turned to disgust as two Council inspectors and the local police have made their first arrest under the punitive anti-Christmas regulations this Council has created. This is Jane Hoffmeyer reporting from the thick of the action, in Plinkbury, England."

All over England, news editors were rubbing their hands in glee. The modest story on the evening news was now turning into an item of global interest. Syndication agencies were hurriedly purchasing copies of the tapes and, within a very short space of time, the activities in Plinkbury town square would be flashed around the world as a lead item. Reporters, on the spot, having spoken once more to Egan, were also hinting that there would be another spectacular event in Plinkbury later in the day.

As the first reports hit the screens of televisions worldwide, three men fainted with shock. The first was Babbo Natale, as the screen in the Yule conference hall spluttered into life and he saw his beloved Ferrari, in a town square in England, with two women draped over it. The second was Santa Claus of England, when he saw what his wife Zazu was wearing, and the third was a Mr Sidney Holland, who was running a fish and chip shop in Wales with his second wife. As he hit the floor, an order of three cod and chips in his hand, he murmured, "That can't be Agnes…" before he lost consciousness.

☆

CHAPTER THIRTEEN

Let There be Light

The residents of Plinkbury began to stir. Years of boredom, disinterest and apathy began to melt away as the first news items came on to the televisions and radios. First, the isolated housewives, many with babies and toddlers, came out of their houses and headed for the town square. The Council had repeatedly refused to fund a town crèche and, although a few enterprising mothers had tried to set up mother and toddler groups, many of the young women had sunk into a mindless routine of staying at home every day and watching television.

The next arrivals were older women, many of whom had recognised Women's Institute members from Nether-Pilsbury, and they had decided to come and lend their voices to the singing.

Soon, it was impossible to move in the square. The sheer press of humanity, most of it female, was trying, in vain, to sing; talk; shop and protest. The staff of the pub had turned up with refreshments for the Nether-Pilsbury protestors and found themselves taking orders for more sandwiches and drinks.

Mr Patel, who, by now, had been under arrest for over an hour, was still in the police car. It had proved impossible to try and move the vehicle. Eventually, having been persuaded that he would not be able to take Mr Patel to the police station, Sergeant Hill had decided to place Mr Patel under 'house arrest' and let him back into his shop, so that he could deal with the many women clamouring to be served. Such was the volume of business that Sergeant Hill found himself helping out behind the shop counter, while the Council inspectors also pitched in by replacing the fast-disappearing stock on the shelves.

Mr Rosenbaum was doing a roaring trade in flashing Christmas earrings and his new dancing partner, Agnes Holland, was assisting him. Zazu, meanwhile, was handing out boxes of Christmas Spirit chocolates to Christine, Nick and Little K and they were pushing through the crowds to dispense them.

None of this latest activity had yet reached the screens of the worldwide news services. The Yule Conference in Finland was still staring in mute astonishment at the interviews that had taken place before lunch.

Babbo Natale had, partially, regained consciousness and kept moaning "Rosa, Rosa." Everyone thought he was asking for his wife, so Mama Rosa was brought down from the wives' viewing gallery to comfort her husband. This she did by cuffing him round the ear and telling him to get a grip on himself.

Santa of England recovered from his faint just in time to see his wife's face fill the screen and say "My name is Zazu Christmas and, because of my name, I've always been a lover of everything to do with Christmas." That made him feel dizzy again and a tomte had to apply some smelling salts.

Pa Kringle had buried his face in his hands but the sound of his daughter's voice made him look at the screen again. As Christine gave her speech (which was really Pa's speech) to the camera, the Yule conference sat in appreciative silence. When she had finished and Jane Hoffmeyer had made her comment about "It takes a child to tell the adults of the world what Christmas really means…," the whole conference stood up, turned to Pa Kringle and began to solemnly applaud. A wave of relief flooded over him. He looked up at the wives' viewing gallery and saw Ma's face, tears streaming down her cheeks. She blew a kiss at him and, for once, without feeling foolish, he blew one back.

The one person who did not feel *at all* happy about the turn of

events in Plinkbury was Ms. Angela Summer, Leader of the
Council. She stood, in impotent fury, watching most of the Council
employees join in the protest. Her hands gripped the wrought-iron
balcony until her knuckles were white. When the front of Mr
Patel's shop lit up, she had to go inside, as she was shaking with rage.

The other members of the Council stood around her, wobbling
with anxiety. She looked at them contemptuously. All of them had
been hand-picked by her for their inability to reach a decision by
themselves. Anyone with any spark of intelligence or opinion had
been manoeuvred out of the Council long ago. Angela Summer
liked to be In Charge and she liked to be A Martyr. She felt that
familiar glow of satisfaction welling up inside her because she was
now going to have to tell everyone what to do.

"Gentlemen!" she bawled. (It should be noted that there were
no other women on Plinkbury Town Council. Angela Summer did
not get on well with other women.) "We need to have an
Emergency Council Meeting!"

Everyone nodded.

"It is now 2.30 p.m. Get yourselves some refreshment; go to the
bathroom; telephone your wives to say you will be late, and
reconvene in this room at 3 p.m." She always treated them like
small children. The men scattered, anxious to do her bidding.

Angela Summer watched the activities in the square from
behind the blinds of the Council Chamber. Her eyes narrowed and
glittered at the escalation of jollity. Someone would pay for this.
She scanned the square. The handsome man had just come out of
his Christmas Shop. Yet more festive goodies were being unloaded
from the truck. How dare he flout her authority in this way! He
obviously thought he was very clever. Ms Summer knew that the
new regulations were worded in such a way that the Council could
only fine shopkeepers who *added* Christmas lights and other
decorations to their premises. However, if the shop in question sold
Christmas lights and decorations all year round, then the Council
were powerless to interfere with the normal business of that shop.

Very clever. She had decided that Mr Egan was going to be made an example of. How she was going to achieve that was another matter.

The first thing to be done was to lock the doors to the Town Hall. Everyone who was inside would have to stay in and everyone who was outside would have to stay out. Ms. Summer allowed herself a malicious smile. She would make the renegade employees in the square cold and miserable. It would be dark soon and the temperature would start to plummet. They would soon stop singing once they were frozen.

Zazu and the three teenagers had managed to make their way into the Christmas Shop to have a meeting with Egan. All the people in the square were now singing *Frosty the Snowman* at the top of their voices.

"What's the next move?" Nick yelled to Egan.

"The lights!" Egan yelled back. "As soon as it gets dark, we'll make an announcement and K and I will throw the lights up. How many do we need, K?"

"Seventy two," K shouted and held up his sketch pad. Everyone looked at his drawing with a smile.

"It should be dark in about twenty minutes," Egan looked at his watch. "Have you got any of the chocolates left?" he yelled at his sister.

"Three boxes," she yelled back. "I don't think we should give out any more. They're too strong!"

"And they're addictive," Christine added loudly. "People are beginning to get aggressive if they can't get any more. I've witnessed a couple of people fighting over them!"

Egan frowned. He would have to go back to Research and Development with this product. Pity. He'd had high hopes.

Mercifully, the singing in the square appeared to have stopped. In fact, it seemed to be strangely quiet.

"OK," Egan said, speaking normally. "K and I will take up our positions, by the Ferrari. You three finish putting the stock out in here. I want to open for business after the lights go on."

As Egan and K stepped out into the square, they realised what had caused the sudden silence. The menacing figure of Ms Angela Summer had appeared on the Council Chamber balcony, her hand raised for attention. Everyone stood there expectantly.

"This display of public disorder is disgraceful!" she shouted to make herself heard to the people at the far end of the square. Pockets of booing broke out and camera crews grinned delightedly at each other.

"What is the Council going to do?" shouted a reporter from the Town Hall steps.

"Are you going to take any action?" shouted another reporter.

"Will the Council reinstate Christmas?"

More reporters called out questions and the people in the square joined in. Everyone was calling out, demanding that Ms Summer make a statement. She held up her hand again and waited for silence.

"The Council will not be intimidated in this manner. We are now going to have an Emergency Council Meeting and, for the duration of that meeting, the Town Hall will be locked. No-one will be allowed to enter or exit. Thank you."

As she disappeared back into the Chamber, there was a surge from the council employees in the square, anxious to get back into the building to get their coats, hats, handbags and umbrellas. But they were too late. As Bella Shuttleworth's singers parted to let them through, they found that the doors had already been locked. They were stuck outside, whether they liked it or not.

Shouted suggestions began to ripple through the crowd.

"Let's climb the walls!"

"Let's set fire to the doors!"

"Let's get a battering ram!"

The last suggestion seemed to find favour with the majority and a large number of them began to push their way back out of the square to find something that they could use as a battering ram.

Egan, sensing that the mood of the crowd had turned ugly, and they needed to be diverted, leant heavily on the Ferrari's horn to get attention. The crowd stopped pushing and looked at him, as he raced up the Town Hall steps.

"Ladies and gentlemen!" he said, turning to face them. "You've been very patient and good-natured today. Let's not spoil it by hasty action. I promised you, this morning, that there would be another phase of our peaceful protest and, if you would all come and gather in the square, facing the Town Hall, we will show you something that you will remember for the rest of your lives."

Murmuring excitedly, the crowd gathered, as instructed, looking expectantly towards Egan. It was almost dark and visibility was poor. K opened the trunk of the car, motioned to Egan, and the two of them grabbed handfuls of K's special lights and threw them towards the Town Hall.

The lights shot upwards, like fireworks. The crowd gasped. The lights whizzed around in the air, until they had each decided on their resting spot, and then they zeroed in and decorated. The crowd went wild. Egan and K threw handful after handful of the multi-coloured lights towards the building. It was the greatest display the people of Plinkbury had ever seen. Streaks of colour were whizzing off in all directions before they chose their spot to drape or swag or swirl. Starting at the left hand side of the building, the lights transformed the dark, forbidding gothic monstrosity of Plinkbury Town Hall into a palace that would easily grace the centre of Las Vegas.

By the time the last light had found its place on the structure, the whole of the town, never mind the square, was bathed in a festive glow. Every balcony of the Town Hall was draped with double swags of lights. The pillars outside the doors were continuous spirals of lights. All the guttering, even the chimneys, were clothed in dazzling colour. It looked like a neon gingerbread house. The crowd roared and cheered and whistled; the cameras clicked and whirred; the reporters gave excitable commentaries to camera. The world was about to view a better light display than the one that was staged at the last Olympic ceremony.

Egan leaned on the car horn again.

"Ladies and gentlemen! I now declare The Christmas Shop of Plinkbury officially open!"

There was a scream of ecstasy from the Valued Customers – a scream that would not have been out of place at a rock concert – and a posse of middle-aged ladies stampeded towards the shop. With a nod from Egan, Zazu unlocked the door, and they streamed in, waving credit cards. Egan was one happy elf.

Mrs Smith, from the bakery, pushed her way through the crowd and tugged at Egan's jacket. He leant over so that she could shout in his ear, then he leant on the horn again.

"Ladies and gentlemen! The bakery has just made a fresh batch of mince pies and they are now selling egg nog to anyone over the age of eighteen!"

Inside the Council Chamber, thanks to K's Christmas lights, it was as bright as a summer's day.

"Is Ernie in the building?" Angela Summer snapped, referring to the Town Hall handyman. Someone thought he might be and they were despatched to find him. Another councillor timidly asked if they could order some tea and coffee and this was allowed by their esteemed Leader. Someone was despatched to find the tea lady.

Ernie, when he was located, was sent out onto the balcony to turn off the offending Christmas lights. But he came back inside, after about twenty minutes, and reported to Ms Summer that he could not find any power source.

"There's no wires, transformers, or plugs," he said incredulously. "Most amazing thing I've ever seen. They can't be switched off!"

"Don't be ridiculous, they must have a power source!" snapped Ms Summer. She was getting quite exasperated. She liked being In Charge but she didn't like it when people couldn't obey her orders.

"They must run on batteries. Just take them down and take them apart!" she ordered, giving Ernie a 'must I do everything ?' look. He sighed and returned to the balcony. It was all very well, saying "take them down," but he couldn't. They just wouldn't be prised off the ironwork. Every time he tried to get a screwdriver underneath one of the ropes of lights, it just slithered up the tool and decorated it. The first time that happened, he had yelped in shock and dropped the screwdriver. The moment it had hit the floor of the balcony, the string of lights just unwound itself and resumed its previous position on the ironwork. The lights were alive.

Ernie decided to treat them like a vermin infestation, so he reached into his toolbox and produced a mallet and tried to hit one. As the mallet came down, the lights just moved out of the way. Ernie went up and down the balcony, manically banging his mallet down and not being able to hit one single string of lights. He got the impression that the lights were actually enjoying the game. He was getting very hot and bothered. The fact that people in the square were laughing at him was not helping. Now the TV cameras were trained on him and he was really getting annoyed.

He pushed his way through the Council members, who had been watching him through the half-open balcony doors.

"It needs drastic action," he said aggressively. "I'll be back in a minute."

"Do you think those lights are magic?" one councillor asked tentatively.

"This is the 21st century," Ms Summer said acidly. "Magic! They're probably being remotely-controlled by somebody standing down in the square, having a good laugh at our expense! Magic!" she looked at the offending councillor with scorn written all over her face and he visibly withered.

Everyone jumped as Ernie returned with a gun.

"Good God, man! Is that a real gun?!!" Ms Summer was taken aback.

"Air gun. Use it to get rid of pigeons off the Town Hall roof. Those lights are vermin, just the same as pigeons." Ernie strode purposefully out on to the balcony.

~138~

He aimed and the shot rang out as it hit the ironwork. Several women in the crowd screamed. Little K and Egan looked up anxiously.

"Will he damage them?" Egan asked with concern.

"I don't know," was K's honest reply.

They needn't have worried. The lights around the balcony, sensing that this was a new threat that required some serious attention, flew off of their decorating positions. One string wrapped itself around the gun and two strings wrapped themselves around Ernie's wrists, effectively handcuffing him. Yet more strings wrapped themselves around his ankles, so that he couldn't walk, and three strings linked together and trussed him up around the chest, pinning his elbows to his sides. The last string of lights, on behalf of them all, smacked Ernie round the face, before settling back on the front of the balcony. He called for help but the cowardly Council members decided that the lights might come into the chamber, so they locked the doors, leaving their helpless handyman tied up outside.

Egan was besieged by reporters, wanting to know more about the amazing lights. He introduced Little K as the inventor but did not allow him to answer any of the questions about the power source.

"These lights were invented so that places, without electrical supplies, could decorate at Christmas or, indeed, any other time of year for any kind of celebration," he said smoothly, anxious to promote the full sales potential of the product. Then he added, "They can only be bought through The Christmas Shop, which is the sole distributor for Living Lights." There, on the spur of the moment, he had given them a name. Living Lights. Egan looked at K. "Living Lights?" as though asking for endorsement. K nodded happily. "Living Lights. Yes."

When the news reports of the Living Lights display reached around the world, the Yule Conference sat in silence for about five minutes. Santa K looked very nervous and got ready to defend himself from any accusations that might arise. No-one could think of anything to say. Then Black Peter came into the Conference Hall and spoke to the Chairman. Old Man Christmas went as white as his beard and spoke.

"Members, it has been reported that our telephone lines are now completely jammed by the Associations of Electrical Manufacturers from all the countries you represent. It is time to devote ourselves to some urgent negotiations. This Emergency Debate is adjourned."

☆

CHAPTER FOURTEEN

A New Development

By 6 p.m. a little light snow had begun to fall and the crowd in Plinkbury town square had begun to thin out a little. Mothers had to take children home to be fed; middle-aged ladies had to go home to feed their husbands and Council employees, having given up any hope of getting back into the Town Hall, were starting to go home - without their coats and hats and, in some cases, without their front door keys. However, almost everyone had decided to come back tomorrow and resume the protest. It was probably the most fun that the people of Plinkbury had had in years.

The Christmas Shop was still a hive of activity, although Harry Allardyce had made it very clear that his bus was going to leave Plinkbury in half an hour. So the Valued Customers and their Women's Institute friends were shopping as fast as they could. Egan had broken out the boxes of American Holiday Dinner Services and was handing them out to everyone. It was a happy band of ladies who finally climbed aboard the bus to head back to Nether-Pilsbury.

The two Council inspectors had decided not to fine Mr Patel for displaying his Christmas lights. After all, the Town Hall was now ablaze with Christmas lights and they could hardly penalise Mr Patel for his insignificant display. Besides, during their stint as shelf-fillers in his shop, they had both eaten liberal amounts of Christmas Spirit chocolates and it was all Mr Patel could do to get them to stop hugging him and go home. Sergeant George Hill decided that he was not going to arrest Mr Patel for being drunk and disorderly because he, quite obviously, wasn't. In fact, George Hill had so much enjoyed serving in Mr Patel's shop for the afternoon, that he was considering becoming a shopkeeper himself, after he retired from the police force. There were one or two empty shops in the square that might do very nicely for what he had in mind.

Not many of Sergeant Hill's colleagues knew that he loved cooking, with a passion. In the back of his mind he had always fancied running a little restaurant and, God knows, he thought, Plinkbury could do with one. A nice little French bistro, where he could whip up some lovely little soufflés and tartes. There were endless possibilities.

George Hill was not the only one who was thinking about the empty shops in the Town Square. Agnes Holland had been turning an idea over and over in her mind all afternoon. The new Agnes Holland discovered that she was not only attractive but sociable as well. Serving in Mr Rosenbaum's jewellers shop had made her realise that she liked talking to people. She particularly liked selling them beautiful things that made their faces light up when they tried them on. She thought about all of Zazu's lovely clothes and how they had filled her with a longing to be beautiful. She would like to give that feeling to some of the women in Plinkbury. Running a dress shop would be wonderful. So much better than running a Bed and Breakfast business. And there was a nice little empty shop next to the jewellers. Right next to her new friend Alvin Rosenbaum, who Agnes had discovered was a widower, a lovely dancer and made her laugh a lot. Yes, she would like to have a business next door to Alvin – then she could keep an eye on him. She would talk to Zazu about it this evening. Zazu would know what to do.

Egan loaded the last of his Valued Customers on to the bus. Many were promising to come back tomorrow, if they could. He blew them all kisses and they squealed with delight. The camera crews were packing up and heading for the pub but many of them stopped and chatted to Egan, just to reassure themselves that there would be some more action tomorrow.

Some camera crews had been told to camp out in the square overnight, in case anything happened. There had been a flurry of interest about 5.30, when the frozen handyman, Ernie, had been rescued from the balcony by the fire brigade. The lights had decided that they didn't want to leave 'the herd', so, as Ernie was grasped by two firemen and lifted over the balcony on to an extendable platform, the lights had detached themselves from him and returned to their original places on the ironwork. Ernie had been wrapped in a thermal blanket and taken away to hospital, shouting curses at the Council for abandoning him to his fate in the freezing cold.

But, since the rescue of Ernie, all had been quiet. The Council had steadfastly refused to open the Town Hall doors. They had sent word, via the tea lady, that they were barricading themselves in for the night. She had relayed the news from an open window on the ground floor. There were no other Council employees in there, apart from her, but she said that she didn't mind staying as she had been promised an overtime payment.

Everyone was shutting up their shops. Mr Patel had made record sales. All his advent calendars had gone, likewise his Christmas cards and wrapping paper. He would have to call in at the Cash and Carry warehouse on his way home and replace the stock.

The bakery still had all its lights ablaze, even though the shop was closed. The hungry crowd in the square had bought everything on Mrs Smith's shelves. She was going to have to bake all through the night, in order to meet the needs of any customers tomorrow.

Mr Rosenbaum had made more money in one day than he had made for the whole of the year – and he had met the charming Agnes Holland. He decided that he would pop all his takings into the night safe at the bank and then escort Agnes home. Agnes had just gone to tell her friends that she would see them later.

Egan, Zazu, Christine, Nick and Little K, sat in a contented huddle in the centre of The Christmas Shop. Today had gone very well but it had been very tiring. They were now rewarding themselves with some cups of hot chocolate.

Zazu appeared from the back of the shop with a tray of mugs.

"You look like you all need some extra energy," she said brightly and she deftly broke the top off a Christmas Spirit chocolate and dropped a little of the amber liquid inside it into each cup.

Egan, whose business brain never stopped ticking over, looked thoughtfully at his sister.

"Doesn't heat affect the Christmas Spirit liquid?" he asked.

Zazu shook her head. "Nothing affects it, as far as I can see. When the Chief Elf was making the first batch, he left a whole trayful outside, by mistake, and they froze. They were like chocolate covered ice cubes, so we all sucked them and they had exactly the same feel-good effect. Try the hot chocolate." She handed round the mugs. Everyone sipped slowly, and felt unusually cheerful after about the third sip.

Egan's cool green eyes lit up.

"That's it! That's how we could market them. Not as chocolates, because they're too strong, but we could freeze dry the liquid and put some granules in individual sachets of hot chocolate! I must call the Chief Elf immediately. We could get the first batch out before Christmas." He rushed off to find his cellphone.

Christine looked out of the window at the Town Hall. It looked glorious, lit up like a fairy palace. If only they could get in and speak to the Council. Pa always said that if you really believed in something, you could persuade another person if you spoke to them face to face. She sipped on her hot chocolate and then, suddenly, she had an idea.

"Listen! Listen, everyone! I've just had a brainwave!"

She was so excited, that everyone stopped chatting and looked at her. Even Egan, clutching his cellphone, came out from the back of the shop to see what was happening.

"The chocolates…in the drink…I know how we can use that!"

"Go on," Nick sounded interested.

"We've got to put it in the Council's tea! Yeah?" Christine looked at everybody, expecting them to say "Yeah! Great idea!" but they didn't.

"Christine, the Council is locked in the Town Hall and we are out here. Just how to we do that?" said Nick patiently.

"Er...duh...we have a flying Ferrari to get us up there..." she pointed at the Town Hall roof "...and we are *Yules* and the Town Hall has *chimneys!*" she gave him a look of amusement. Boys could be so dense!

Nick flushed but Little K said excitedly, "Transmogrification! Yes. We could do it!"

Egan held a restraining hand up.

"Hold on, hold on," he said carefully, "What you are proposing is that you fly up on to the Town Hall roof in the Ferrari. Point One – where do you park a Ferrari on a roof like that?" They all looked up at the Town Hall. There was not a flat piece of roof in sight. "Then...then, you propose to transmogrify down the chimneys, so that you are in the Town Hall, and put Christmas Spirit in the Council's tea. Is that right?"

Christine and Little K nodded.

Egan looked at them both. "Do you know, I think you could do it!" He laughed. "It's crazy but I think you could. But..." he added "I would have to fly the car up there and hover, so that you three could get out, and then bring it back down again. You could let yourselves out through the front doors."

Nick had gone strangely quiet and Zazu had noticed, as only a mother would. She knew what his problem was and she knew how to solve it.

"Nick's the only one who really knows how to drive the car," she said firmly. "Perhaps he should be the driver and Christine and K go down the chimneys."

Christine realised that Nick had been put in an embarrassing position. She had forgotten that he had difficulty transmogrifying and she suddenly felt very guilty.

"Yes, of course," she added hastily, "Nick would have to be the driver. That's the best idea." She noticed the relief flood into Nick's face and she smiled.

"Oh, I'm not sure…" Egan said doubtfully. He was really anxious to get behind the wheel of the Ferrari himself but he trailed off in mid sentence as he felt the full force of Zazu's glare.

"No, Egan," Zazu was very firm. "You and I have got to get the camera crews out of the square, somehow. I don't know how we're going to do it but we have to get them all away, so that the car can be flown."

"Yes, you're right," Egan conceded.

Little K had another thought. "We also need to make sure that we go down the right chimney. We don't want to appear in the Council Chamber. We need to see a plan of the Town Hall really."

"Is there a library here?" Egan asked. "Did anyone see a library?"

"Yes," Nick volunteered. "I saw one in the street near the pub. It was only small though."

"Libraries often have plans of public buildings. What's the time?" Egan frantically looked at his watch. "5.45. We may be too late. Quick!"

Everyone hurtled out of the shop and began running down the side street towards the library. All except Zazu, who never ran anywhere, due to her love of unsuitable shoes.

They reached the library doors and the lights were still on.

"Look! Look!" Christine pointed at the sign by the door. "It doesn't close until 6 on a Friday. We've just made it!" And they all tumbled through the doors.

Plinkbury Library was a very old little building. It had been endowed by a local businessman in 1892 and it had been the town's pride and joy for the first half of the twentieth century. Its wood panelling and marble floors spoke of a proud era of literacy and public benefaction. It had been much-used by the citizens of Plinkbury until the advent of the computer age. Then, a refusal by the Council to invest in new technology had left the library in the position of being little more than a museum. Molly Peters had been the librarian in charge for over thirty years and, during that time, her heart had been broken by the attitude of the Council. Ms Angela Summer had tried, on more than one occasion, to have the library closed down, declaring it "an unnecessary drain on resources." Molly Peters had defended her library fiercely. She had managed to get her regular borrowers to sign petitions. She had moved swiftly to have the building listed as a historic monument. But she knew that she was fighting a losing battle. Eventually, the Council would have their way and close the library down. She had heard rumours that Ms Summer wanted to turn it into a Council Chamber. The last thing that the town of Plinkbury needed was another Council Chamber! What it needed were more public amenities, like an up-to-date library and a regular programme of library events.

The abrupt arrival of a man and three teenagers was, therefore, somewhat of a shock to Molly. She was just about to put her coat on and go home.

"The library closes in ten minutes," she said in a helpful tone of voice. She would never turn away people who were genuinely in need of the library services.

"Oh thank you," Egan was slightly out of breath. "We were wondering…do you keep plans of the Town Hall?"

"Well…yes…as a matter of fact we do," Molly's interest was aroused. "Follow me."

She took them to a large wooden plan chest at the back of the library and opened the third drawer down.

"All the Town Hall plans are in there. Please make sure that your hands are clean and dry."

Everyone looked at their hands and then rubbed them on their trousers. Then they went into an excited huddle over the plans.

Molly withdrew to a discreet distance. It was the policy of all good librarians never to eavesdrop on people's research. She looked again at the group. They seemed familiar. It was when they were joined by a glamorous woman wearing an elf outfit that she realised they were the people she had seen on the small television in her office. In fact, she had been riveted all day by the protest in the square. These were the people who had taken on Ms Angela Summer and appeared to be winning, at the moment. She wondered if she could confide an important piece of information to them. Information that she had been waiting a very long time to give to someone.

She cleared her throat.

"Huh..hmm. Excuse me…"

They all looked up from the plans.

"Are you the organisers of today's protest?" she asked, directing her question at Egan.

He nodded. "Yes, I suppose we are."

Molly took her courage in both hands and asked another question.

"Will you be resuming the protest tomorrow?"

Egan straightened up, his inbuilt radar was humming. This woman looked like she wanted to help them, in some way.

"We are hoping to," he answered, "Why?"

"I have something very important that I would like to show you," Molly said, lowering her voice conspiratorially. "Could you follow me?"

Intrigued, the group followed the librarian to her office. She went to her desk and took a pair of white cotton gloves out of a drawer. Then she picked up a small key.

"The archives are just over here," she said, motioning them towards a large cabinet. She unlocked a set of doors and slid out a shelf, then, very carefully, lifted down what looked like a parchment.

"You see the Council are such ignorant people. They have no idea of this town's history – nor do they care." Two little pink spots of anger appeared on Molly Peter's cheeks. Just talking about the Council raised her blood pressure within seconds.

"This document…" she continued "is a Royal Charter. Elizabeth the First gave the Town of Plinkbury the right to hold a market in the square on one Saturday every month. But it has to be a Saturday that falls on or near a saint's day. Tomorrow is Saturday December 2nd. Which is very close to December 6th, which is…"

"St. Nicholas' Day!" everyone chorused with glee.

"Quite!" she was quite excited and happy now. "This Royal Charter has never been revoked and the Council don't appear to know about it. It means that a market could quite legally be held in the square tomorrow and there is nothing they could do about it."

"Excellent!" Egan breathed, his mind working overtime. He would have to make lots and lots of phone calls but he was pretty sure that he could successfully whip up a busy market for tomorrow morning. Lots of people owed him favours. "Would you be willing to stay open for, say, another hour, so that we could bring the media in here and explain to them about the charter?"

"Oh yes! I'd be very happy to do that!" Molly Peters was thrilled. At last she was going to get an opportunity to pay back the Council for all the years of neglect and harassment.

"And could we possibly photocopy the Charter, so that we can put the copy up in the square, for the benefit of the police and the Council?"

"Yes, yes. I can organise that immediately."

"Absolutely wonderful, Mrs…er.." Egan groped for her name.

"Peters. Molly Peters."

"Molly Peters, you are an angel," and Egan took her white-gloved hand and planted one of his chivalrous kisses on it. Molly's knees trembled slightly.

Back in the Christmas Shop, the gang organised themselves.

"OK," Egan was taking charge again. "Christine, K and Nick, you wait by the Ferrari until the square is absolutely empty. Zazu, you act as look-out. Stand at the corner of the square and make sure that all the reporters have gone into the library and then you give a signal to the kids."

"Gotcha," Zazu giggled and gave a thumbs-up.

"Meanwhile," Egan continued, "I will go and round up the media and take them to see Molly Peters. Kids, you know which chimneys to target, yes?"

Little K spoke from his photographic memory, "Yes. The third and fourth chimneys on the far right of the building will give us entry into the offices at the back."

Egan looked at Christine. "Have you got your supply of chocolates?"

Christine plunged both hands into her coat pockets and pulled out two fistfuls of chocolates.

"Good. OK. Good luck everyone and here we go."

The gang came out of the shop and scattered. Christine, Nick and Little K took up their positions by the Ferrari, while Zazu and Egan split up and went to talk to the various media crews. It was working. Cameras were loaded with tapes, microphones were picked up and other equipment was hoisted over shoulders. Pretty soon, everyone was following Egan down the side street towards the library. Zazu took up her position as look-out.

She gave them the thumbs-up and they climbed into the car. Nick put the gear lever into F, gently depressed the accelerator and the car glided upwards. He turned the wheel slightly to the left and the car turned upwards and round until it was above the Town Hall roof.

"Those two chimneys there!" said Little K pointing ahead.

Nick depressed the brake slightly and the car hovered.

"Down a bit," Christine pleaded. She wasn't about to jump five feet onto a sloping roof. Nick manoeuvred as best he could. Christine and Little K clambered out and gingerly placed their feet on the roof tiles. They both fell forwards and grasped the apex of the roof and clung there.

"We're OK!" Little K called up to Nick and he nodded, before gliding upwards. He circled twice, to make sure that his friends had found their footing on the roof and were both standing by the relevant chimneys, before gliding slowly down to the resting place in front of the Town Hall.

The chimneys were tall, but not too tall. Christine clambered up the side of hers and sat on its rim, her feet dangling into the blackness. Little K did the same on his chimney. The two friends

looked at each other and smiled.

"Ready?" Christine asked.

K nodded and smiled.

Christine closed her eyes, muttered "Merry Christmas to one and all," and jumped. She felt the familiar, giddy rush as her body exploded into a thousand atoms. Zazu, watching closely from the street below, saw the two puffs of glittery, red dust from the chimneys and she knew that both children had successfully transmogrified. She let out a long breath of relief and waved at Nick. He cut the car engine and waited for his friends to successfully complete their mission.

☆

CHAPTER FIFTEEN

Christmas Spirit by the Cupful

The curious thing about Transmogrification is that, although you don't have a body, as such, while you are hurtling down a chimney, you feel as though you have one. So Christine could feel the sides of the chimney rushing past her arms and shoulders and she could feel her hair flying upwards as she descended. The sensation, for her, was rather like going down a vertical drop slide. Her stomach seemed to have been temporarily left behind. Pa Kringle said that you got used to it. After all, he did it hundreds of thousands of times every Christmas Eve - although he always felt a little queasy at the end of the night. Christine was still a teenager and Transmogrification was a newly acquired skill so, for her, the experience was still intense.

The good thing about transmogrifying, if it was done correctly, was that a Yule body was able to sense when the chimney was opening up to a fireplace, so the speed of descent automatically slowed. Christine was able to drop the last few feet quite slowly, so that there was very little impact when her feet touched the floor. Then – and this was the part of the process that many Yule teenagers had difficulty with – you had to go into a crouching position, so that when your body re-materialised, your head and shoulders wouldn't still be inside the chimney. Many a young Yule had forgotten that bit, stepped forward, with their eyes shut, and smacked into the chimney wall. Black eyes and the odd broken nose were common amongst first-timers.

The moment that Christine's feet touched the floor and she went into the crouching position, her body became whole again. She looked at her hands and felt her hair. Not a speck of soot. Excellent. That had been a good transit.

Fortunately, there was no fire. It was what was known in the trade as a 'dead fireplace'. Christine had only had one attempt at transmogrifying into a live fireplace and it hadn't worked very well. What was supposed to happen was that as soon as the feet sensed the warmth of smoke in the chimney, the body atoms shifted to the front of the chimney stack, filtered along the bricks, funnelled out of the fireplace (avoiding the flames) and re-materialised in front of the fireplace. When Christine had tried it, she had panicked and shot straight back up the chimney, re-materialising back on the roof. The main thing with the Transmogrification was not to panic, otherwise the whole process would reverse. It was no wonder that Nick, with his fifty percent elf genes, found it difficult.

There was also the problem of houses with no fireplace. Christine knew that, next year, she would have to practice transmogrifying through glass, because houses with no fireplaces had to be entered through windows. Going through glass required a whole different technique.

Anyway, there she was, safely down the chimney and standing upright in front of the fireplace. The large office was bathed in the glow from the Living Lights outside and she could find her way quite easily to the door. Now to find Little K, who should be in the next room.

When she entered, she could hear muffled sounds of distress. Her heart leapt. Supposing Little K's Transmogrification had gone wrong? What would she do? She frantically tried to remember her transmogrifying first aid classes. Where was the fireplace? Another moment of panic! Perhaps it had been bricked up!

The sounds were coming from behind a row of metal filing cabinets and Christine realised, with relief, the cabinets were in front of the fireplace.

"K! Can you hear me? K!" she said anxiously.

"Yes!" came the muffled answer. "It's all dark in here. I can't get out!"

"There's a row of filing cabinets in front of the fireplace. Are you OK? Have you re-materialised?"

"Yes. I'm fine, I think. But I can't get out!"

"I'll try and move something," Christine said helpfully.

She tugged and pulled but the four drawer cabinets were just too heavy – full, as they were, with documents.

"I can't shift them," she said, panting a little, "You'll have to reverse the process. Go back out on to the roof and come down my chimney."

There was a silence.

"K? Did you hear me?"

"Yes. I heard you. But I don't think I can do it. I feel a bit sick."

Christine felt so sorry for him, trapped in a chimney, in the dark. She always expected everyone to be as comfortable with the Transmogrification as she was. K was too young to handle emergency procedures.

"Don't worry. I'll get help. Hang on!"

There was only one thing to do. She was going to have to creep out of the front door and get Nick and Zazu.

"Don't panic K. I'll be back in a little while," she said reassuringly.

Christine made her way, quietly, down the corridor. Fortunately, there was no-one about. She could hear raised voices coming from the floor below – presumably the Council Chamber. She looked down the stair well. She was three floors up. There was bound to be someone between here and the front door.

She gingerly walked down the stairs to the next floor. There was still no-one in sight. She couldn't resist listening at the door of the Council Chamber.

"This situation requires firm measures. We cannot let these

people flout the regulations like this." Ms Summer was loud and angry.

"But no-one, so far, has contravened the regulations, except the newsagent," a man's voice replied timidly.

"Then we must make new regulations!" Ms Summer was not to be swayed from her vendetta against the festive season. "We must get that Christmas Shop closed down at once."

"But I don't see how…" another timid man spoke.

"Well you'd better get your thinking caps on, hadn't you?" Ms Summer interrupted harshly. "Because, gentlemen, we are going to find a way to put a stop to this, if it takes us all night!"

There were some sighs and mild objections from the Council members but it was obvious to the listening Christine that they were all too scared of their Leader to really make a stand.

She tiptoed down the next flight of stairs and heard someone humming. It was the tea lady in the kitchen which, judging by the sound of clinking china and the smell of warm steam, was somewhere to the left of the staircase. Christine carried on down the next flight of stairs and scuttled towards the large front doors.

She silently opened the door and peered out. Zazu and Nick were sitting in the Ferrari, trying to keep warm. Christine managed to catch Nick's eye and frantically motioned him to come over.

"Have you finished already?" Nick asked with a grin.

"No!" Christine hissed. "We haven't even started. K's trapped in the chimney and I need your help!"

The grin faded from Nick's face and he ran back to the car to get his mother. Christine ushered them both into the Town Hall and put her finger to her lips to caution them to be silent.

"Two flights up" she whispered. "Follow me."

Zazu took off her stiletto boots and padded, barefoot, behind the two teenagers. Carefully, they made their way up the flights of stairs, stopping at each level to make sure that the tea lady was still in her kitchen and the Council was still in its Chamber.

"This is it," Christine opened the door. "K! Are you OK? I've brought help!"

"Yes. I'm feeling better now, thank you," came the muffled reply.

The three of them tugged and pulled at the filing cabinet and, eventually, managed to shift it by about a foot. Christine clambered up on to the top and peered over. Little K was sitting, curled up on the fireplace floor.

"You'll have to come over the top of the cabinet. Give me your hands," she instructed.

Christine grasped K's hands and pulled, while he scrabbled with his feet, his trainers sticking, helpfully, to the metal of the cabinet. Soon, he was far enough up to haul himself over the top. They both dropped down onto the floor. Little K was very sooty.

"Thank you my friends," he said gratefully. "I did not know how I was going to get out of there. I am not good at transmogrifying upwards."

Nick slapped him on the back and a small cloud of soot puffed into the air. "I know just how you feel, man," he said sympathetically.

Zazu produced a handkerchief, did the 'mother thing' of making K spit on it and then she cleaned his face up a bit. "I knew this whole thing would be too much for you children," she said anxiously.

"Mum, it's cool. Just leave it," Nick was embarrassed again.

"Anyway, we'd better get on with spiking the tea," Christine said urgently. "I just overheard that dreadful woman say that they are going to make new regulations and close down The Christmas Shop."

Zazu tutted. "That woman could do with a good makeover."

Christine wasn't sure whether she meant beautifying or being beaten up, but it didn't matter.

"I know where the kitchen is but how are we going to get the tea lady out of there?" Christine asked and everyone frowned.

"Some sort of diversion?" said Nick.

Christine was exasperated. "Well obviously! But what?"

"I could cut the power," Little K offered.

Christine shook her head. "No. That would bring the councillors out of the Council Chamber. We don't want that."

"I could distract her," Zazu said brightly.

"How?" Christine looked doubtful.

"Well, I bet she doesn't know everyone who works in this building. I could pretend to be a council worker, desperate for a cup of tea."

"Mum, you're dressed like an elf." Nick thought he ought to point out the obvious.

Zazu giggled. "So I am! Well how about if I put that on?" she pointed to a raincoat hanging on a hook behind the door. It probably belonged to one of the council workers locked out of the Town Hall earlier. She put on the raincoat, took off her elf hat and looked reasonably presentable.

Christine was beginning to feel hopeful. "OK, that's good. But you have to get her *out* of the kitchen for a few minutes."

Zazu looked around and her eye lighted upon an electric fire. "I could ask her to come here and show me how the fire works. I could pretend to be dumb, you know…like I don't know how to do anything."

The three teenagers smiled and looked at each other. Bless her, Zazu certainly knew how to act dumb.

"OK! I think we have a workable plan here! Let's go!" Christine led the way down to the kitchen.

The three friends hid in the room next to the kitchen and held the door slightly open, so that they could see when Zazu passed by with the tea lady. Zazu strolled, in bare feet, to the kitchen door.

"Excuse me…" she said and the tea lady let out a yelp of shock.

"Ooh my goodness, you gave me a fright! I thought there was no-one else left in the building!"

"Oh, I'm so sorry!" Zazu put on her best helpless voice. "I only just started here today. Fancy! My first day and I get locked in! I'm desperate for a cup of tea and I can't get the fire in my office to work. Do you think you could help me?"

The tea lady came over all motherly. Such a pretty thing and not a brain in her head! Of course she would help her!

"You poor love! I don't know what this council are playing at, I really don't. Locking young girls in the Town Hall overnight. You make sure you get overtime for this inconvenience, dear."

Zazu assured her that she would.

"I'll make you a nice cup of tea and we'll take it along to your office and sort out your fire for you," the tea lady said reassuringly.

She prattled on, while the kettle was boiling. "If anyone was to ask me, I'd say that the whole lot of them councillors should be sacked for the way they've let this town run down. It's a disgrace. I don't know what they do with the council's money but they certainly don't spend it on improving the lot of people who live here…" On and on she went. Christine began to feel that this could be a long night.

Finally, Zazu and the tea lady set off for the office to sort out the electric fire.

Quick as a flash, the three friends ran into the kitchen and Christine began digging chocolates out of her pockets.

"Right. You two spike the tea urn and I'll do the coffee pot," she whispered.

They all began unwrapping the chocolates and breaking the tops off.

"How many do you think, for the urn?" Nick asked

Christine pulled a face. "It's awfully big."

"Two gallon capacity," said Little K, reading off the side of the ancient contraption. "I calculate ten chocolates for maximum effect."

"How many for the coffee pot?" Christine asked, deferring to K's superior scientific knowledge.

"Four." K seemed definite, so four it would be.

"Let's hope it works," Nick said, voicing the concern that everyone was feeling, as they left the kitchen and hid once more.

After what seemed like an age, the tea lady passed by again and went back to reading her magazine. They emerged and tiptoed down the stairs. Zazu was waiting for them by the front doors. They peered out and, as there was still no-one in the square, they left the building, gently closing the great door behind them.

Back in the warmth of The Christmas Shop, Egan looked very pleased with himself.

"Well, that will be the major news item tomorrow," he said triumphantly. "The Royal Charter that no-one knew about and the St.Nicholas Market that is going to take place here."

"How are you going to organise that then?" Christine was the first with her question, as usual.

Egan brandished his cellphone. "I've already called my friend, the Christmas tree grower, because Little K said we needed a big Christmas tree in the square to get the lights off of the Town Hall. I have also called my friend the mistletoe grower, who is, as we speak, loading up his truck with branches of mistletoe and a market stall, so that he can set up here in the morning. I shall now call several more friends. For example, the lady who makes holly wreaths, the lady who makes Christmas tree angels, another who makes wooden Christmas mobiles and so on. If you'll excuse me, I have a lot of calls to make."

"Do you think they will all come?" Zazu asked.

Egan smiled broadly. "Does Santa have a white beard? The free publicity generated by the Plinkbury protest is worth a king's ransom. Of course they will come. Tomorrow, this place will look like a Christmas market in Disneyland. Trust me."

Everyone smiled and Zazu made some more hot chocolate. It was getting late and they were all tired. News reporters began filtering back to the square from the library. They were all excited about this new development. The footage they had shot tonight would be held over so that they could add on scenes of the promised Christmas market in the morning.

Christine looked up at the Town Hall. Hopefully, the Council members would be drinking the first of their many cups of tea and coffee right now. Things could be very interesting tomorrow.

☆

CHAPTER SIXTEEN

Publicity worth a King's Ransom

The greatest surprise for the members of the Yule Conference was that, when they took the telephone calls from the Electrical Manufacturer's Associations, everybody *loved* the Living Lights. They had suspected that the lights were something to do with the Yule Dynasty and they all wanted to manufacture them under licence.

One manufacturer who did not ring, however, was a very single-minded man in England, called Terry Madeley. He believed in direct action – not exploratory phone calls. Madeley had recently bought out the old family-run firm of Egertons, knowing that the firm had special contracts with the Yule Dynasty. The Egerton family were useless businessmen. If it hadn't been for their special Christmas contracts to manufacture electronic components for interactive toys, the company would have gone bust years ago. Madeley was looking to build on those Yule contracts. When he saw the first television news items of the Living Lights working their magic on Plinkbury Town Hall, he decided to drive through the night, contract in his pocket, and get a piece of the action.

When he arrive in Plinkbury, it was five 'o'clock in the morning. Very little was stirring, except the newsagents, which was taking delivery of the day's newspapers. The television and radio vans were there, all locked up and the Town Hall was ablaze with the Christmas lights, fiercely illuminating the dark, winter morning. There had been a covering of snow overnight and the whole scene looked magical.

Madeley parked his car in a side street and walked over to the Town Hall. He touched some of the lights and noted how cool they were, even though they had been alight for many hours and how they quivered when he touched them, a bit like an animal being stroked. He was a ruthless man, not given to enthusiasm, but even he felt some faint stirrings as he examined the lights in minute detail. No discernible power source. If there were batteries inside the lights, he could not see how they had been inserted. It was every electrical manufacturer's dream, to make a product that would be entirely safe for children to handle. No toddlers electrocuting themselves by sticking their fingers in sockets. No fires caused by overheating Christmas tree lights. He began to feel a tension and warmth in his face – the nearest he ever came to excitement. He wanted this contract so much, that it hurt.

Back in Finland, the Yule Dynasty had wisely decided to defer to Santa K over the matter of manufacturing licences. He was, after all, the father of the inventor. It had to be his decision as to which companies would be awarded contracts. However, that did not stop them besieging him with ideas, suggestions and requests. Dun Lao Chen of China had been first off the mark, showing Santa K a list of suitable Chinese manufacturers who should be considered and promising that the Chinese could undercut any price that anyone else offered. Babbo Natale was also fairly aggressive in his lobbying of Santa K. Certain Italian manufacturers made it very clear to him that they would be very upset if he did not get the contract for them.

So it was with some relief that Santa K took delivery of an email from Egan, offering to be the sole European distributor of the Living Lights and to also select manufacturers that he personally trusted. Santa K dictated a grateful reply to a tomte in the administration offices saying that, as far as he was concerned, Egan could have *World* distribution rights and deal with *all* the manufacturers. That should get the Yule Dynasty off his back for a while.

Egan had not slept all night. First he had organised people to come to the market with their products, then he had e-mailed Little K's father with the offer of distribution. He was ecstatic when Santa K's reply came back. *World* distribution rights! Excellent! He sent an email accepting and promising that the necessary paperwork would follow shortly. He would have to wait until The Christmas Shop down south opened, before he could get his secretary to type up a contract.

At six o'clock in the morning, the first market vendors began to arrive. Egan took a large swig of coffee and set about organising the positions of stalls. He had read and re-read the copy of the Royal Charter and was delighted to find that it even allowed for the sale of ale and wine, so he had telephoned a friend and organised a mulled wine and ale stall. This he would place next to the Town Hall steps. The fumes of sweet spices should bring the Council members out on to the balcony.

When the bleary-eyed media crews began to arrive, the square was filling up with stalls. Trucks were unloading mountains of holly and mistletoe and someone had set up some speakers, so that Christmas music could be played at the appropriate time. Egan had, rather cheekily, pinned the copy of the Royal Charter to the Town Hall doors, for all to read – particularly the police, should they turn up.

At seven o'clock, the Ferrari glided into the square and Zazu, Agnes, Christine, Nick and Little K began unloading armfuls of clothes.

"Agnes is going to set up a shop, today," Zazu informed her brother as she pushed through The Christmas Shop door, both hands full of dresses on hangers. "We're just going to put all these clothes in your stock room until the real estate agency opens and Agnes can sign a lease."

Egan's eyebrows shot up. "Where, may I ask, did all those clothes come from?" he asked.

"I drove Mum home last night and she emptied out her dressing room," said Nick, as he staggered past with another armful.

"I was bored with these clothes anyway," said Zazu over her shoulder as she left the shop, "and the women in this town need them more than I do."

Egan was stunned. Agnes came through with yet more clothes, followed by Christine, with another armful.

"There won't be enough space in my stock room!" Egan protested to his sister, as she passed with bags full of shoes.

"It's only for a couple of hours, don't be boring," Zazu always got her own way. Egan sighed. However irritating it was for him, it wasn't half as bad as it was going to be for Zazu's husband – who was going to have to buy her a whole new wardrobe.

By eight o'clock, the market was complete and the stallholders were happily arranging and decorating their stalls. Mrs Smith, from the bakery, worn out from her night's baking, decided to open up early and was doing a roaring trade in warm croissants and steaming coffee. Mr Patel usually opened at eight, anyway, and was gleefully selling newspapers as fast as he could undo the bundles.

By half past eight, the first of the Council employees arrived, hoping that they could get into their place of work, but the doors remained firmly locked. So they occupied themselves by eating and drinking and reading the Royal Charter with interest.

Just before nine o'clock, it was decided that the market would be officially opened. Egan was asked to make the announcement, so that it could be captured on film. The Sky reporter took up her position.

"This is Jane Hoffmeyer reporting from the town of Plinkbury in England where the people's protest against the Christmas ban has entered its second day. There has been a new development in the campaign. A Royal Charter, no less, has been discovered. It seems that Queen Elizabeth the First took time off from fighting the Spanish Empire to grant the town of Plinkbury the right to hold a street market on one Saturday in every month. That Saturday has to be the nearest one to a saint's day. Today is December 2nd and

St.Nicholas, the patron saint associated with Christmas, has his saint's day on December 6th. So Plinkbury is now going to hold an annual St. Nicholas Market every December. It seems that the Council didn't know about the Charter but, so far, they are still locked in the Town Hall and have declined to comment. Meanwhile, a perfectly legal Christmas market is taking place, right in front of them and, it appears, there is nothing they can do about it."

The Town Hall clock struck nine and Egan shouted "I now declare Plinkbury's St Nicholas Market officially open!" A cheer went up from the crowd and Christmas music began to blare out of the speakers. Cameras whirred and TV crews began to pan up and down the stalls.

Angela Summer awoke with a jolt. Someone was playing *Deck the Halls with Boughs of Holly* very loudly, outside the window. She looked around. All the other Council members were beginning to awake from their strange positions in various chairs, on the floor, or on the large Council meeting table. It had been a very odd meeting last night. After numerous cups of tea and coffee and heated lectures from Ms Summer, the meeting had suddenly degenerated into a Christmas sing-song. The tea lady had appeared, wearing tinsel in her hair, and singing *I saw Mummy Kissing Santa Claus*. Despite herself, Angela Summer had found herself laughing and joining in. It wasn't like her at all. Her mouth felt like the bottom of a budgerigar's cage, so she took a swig of cold coffee and tried to pull herself together. The room smelt of sweaty socks and old carpets. Some air was needed.

As Ms Summer opened the balcony windows and stepped out, a shout went up from the reporters, who had been watching the Town Hall, hopefully, for some signs of life. They were calling questions out to her but she couldn't hear them for the noise of the music over the loudspeakers. All she could do was gape in open-mouthed astonishment at the scene before her. There was a large market in the square! There were people streaming into the end of the square and rushing from stall to stall. She could smell something distinctly...well...Christmassy and she looked down below the balcony. To her horror there were people selling mulled wine by the Town Hall steps! This had to be stopped!

She stepped back into the Council Chamber and lifted up the telephone receiver.

"I'm going to call the police! There are about forty three regulations being broken in the square and I'm going to put a stop to it, once and for all!" she barked, to no-one in particular.

All the other Council members took their turn surveying the scene in the square outside. Some of them began laughing - those who had drunk the most tea the night before were still feeling the effects.

"Mulled wine!" cried one.

"Gingerbread men!" spotted another.

"Croissants!" said a third.

The starving councillors headed for the door.

"Stop! Come back here at once!" Ms Summer interrupted her rant at the Worcestershire County Police to try and stop the mass defection but they took no notice. The room was soon empty, save for the tea lady, who was just beginning to wake up.

"You!" Ms Summer shouted rudely at the half-awake woman, "get me a strong cup of tea at once!"

Muttering sullenly, the tea lady tottered out of the Council Chamber and back to her kitchen. Strong tea! I'll give her strong tea! She thought to herself, resentfully. She can have last night's tea warmed up again! That should be nice and stewed! And she poured all the dregs from half-empty cups back into the pot and put it on the electric ring to heat up again.

The councillors had hurtled out of the Town Hall doors like men possessed. They made a beeline for the any stalls that were selling food and drink. News reporters tried to interview them but they had their mouths too stuffed with mince pies, gingerbread, croissants and bagels to be able to answer coherently.

"So what is the Council's response to the discovery of The Royal Charter?" said one reporter.

"Mmrr Jrrer?" replied a councillor, his eyebrows raised in query.

"How will the council tackle this new development, given that the market appears to be perfectly legal?" the reporter persisted.

"Miimm Dnnmm!" the councillor shrugged his shoulders with indifference.

"Thank you," the reporter decided to forget the whole thing and find someone else to interview.

It was now half past nine and Agnes Holland had taken over the lease of the empty shop next to Alvin Rosenbaum. Zazu and Christine were hanging up clothes and dressing the window. The women of Plinkbury began to stop and stare. Gorgeous clothes!

Sequinned evening bags! Impossibly high-heeled shoes! A queue began to form.

When the police arrived, there was nowhere to park. The square was jammed with festive shoppers, all laughing; eating; drinking and making merry. The loudspeakers were playing *Have a Holly, Jolly Christmas*, with ear -splitting clarity. The police parked their two cars in a nearby street and struggled through to the Town Hall. Egan, having left Little K and Nick in charge of The Christmas Shop, was waiting for them on the steps.

"I'm sorry you've been called out unnecessarily, gentlemen," he said smoothly, "If you would just read this, I think you will find that everything is in order."

The senior policeman of the group put on a pair of spectacles and began reading the Charter with interest. The other policemen just smiled and looked bemused. Angela Summer leaned out over the balcony and screamed "Arrest them! Arrest them!" but no-one heard her - the music was just too loud.

Her head was aching and the tea lady had returned with "fresh" tea, so Ms Summer conceded defeat, temporarily, and retreated to partake of several strong cups before launching a fresh attack on the festive troublemakers.

The police just shrugged at Egan and filtered off into the crowd.

"The wife wants me to get a wreath for the front door," said one policeman, apologetically.

Terry Madeley had been watching everything with interest and judged that now was the best time to approach the man he had seen on television – the one who seemed to be the ring leader.

"Madeley," he said, offering his hand to Egan, "owner of Egerton Electronics. I'm interested in manufacturing these Living Lights. I've got a contract in my pocket and I want to talk business."

Egan smiled. This was obviously a man who knew his own mind.

"We'll find somewhere quiet to talk," he said, leading the way towards The Christmas Shop.

Further along the square, Agnes Holland's new shop was full to capacity. This was mostly due to Zazu, who was enthusiastically advising customers on hair and make-up, while they selected their clothes. Dowdy women were coming into the shop and leaving transformed. Husbands, who had waited for them, conveniently, at the mulled wine and ale stall, were very pleasantly surprised when their wives re-appeared. It was either the effect of the drink or someone was working magic on the women of Plinkbury!

Alvin Rosenbaum was very impressed. Most of the customers from Agnes' shop were coming straight into his shop to buy that extra-special piece of jewellery to finish off their new outfits. Agnes and he could become a formidable partnership, he thought to himself, happily.

In the back office of The Christmas Shop, Terry Madeley was trying to convince Egan that he would be the best person in England to manufacture Living Lights. Egan was playing it cool. He knew, from Santa K's e-mail, that *all* the electrical manufacturers in the world were falling over themselves to get a licence to manufacture these lights. Terry Madeley would have to come up with a really good offer to clinch the deal. However, he was first off the mark, which counted for something. It showed great determination. Egan decided to put him through a little test.

"Excuse me one moment," he said and stepped out into the shop.

Little K and Nick were very busy serving eager customers but he wanted them to sit in on the business meeting. However, the problem was solved by the appearance of Bella Shuttleworth, Egan's Most Valued Customer and her husband. They would be perfect shop assistants! Egan smiled and moved towards them.

Angela Summer was beginning to feel very light headed indeed. After several cups of tea, she felt an irresistible urge to sing along to the current song that was booming out of the loudspeakers.

"Silver bells.." she trilled *"Silver bells....It's Christmas time in*

the city...."

"*Ding a ling,*" the tea lady had appeared and was joining in, "*Hear them ring,*"

"*Soon it will be Christmas day...*" they managed, between them, a perfect pitch harmony on the last line, which sent them both into fits of giggles.

"Have a mince pie!" said the tea lady, brandishing a plateful.

"Don't mind if I do!" Angela Summer remembered that she was, actually, very hungry.

"Now, tell me Your Worship..." the tea lady was beginning to feel quite reckless and she'd only had two cups of strong tea, "you can tell old Enid...what's all this nonsense about banning Christmas? What's it in aid of, eh?"

Angela Summer looked at Enid and she felt her eyes filling up with tears. Enid looked like a kind soul. A motherly soul. Ms Summer began to tell the tea lady a sad tale of many Decembers without any Christmas cheer.

Angela Summer's parents had both been university professors. Her father's subject had been Applied Mathematics and her mother's had been Logic. Both had been utterly determined to remove any magic from their only child's life at a very early age. Angela told Enid how, at the age of seven, she had been summoned to stand before her parents.

"Angela Mary," her mother had started. She always called her by both her forenames but never explained why. "It is time that you put away childish things and became more mature."

"Yes," her father had agreed. "Starting tomorrow, we shall give your dolls away to the local hospital and you shall start a course of home tutoring in philosophy."

Angela had cried, for the last time. Crying was childish as well, she was informed. Grown up people didn't cry.

Then her parents told her that Santa Claus was a myth and didn't really exist. That was when her heart was broken.

"All such things are myths, invented to amuse children, and, at some point, you have to put them behind you and learn about real things in life." Her mother had been firm and unmoving.

"What about the Tooth Fairy?" Angela had asked tremulously, wobbling her front tooth as she spoke.

"Poppycock," said her father, with a disapproving look on his face.

"Balderdash," echoed her mother. "No such thing."

"The Easter Bunny?" It had been one faint last hope.

"Stuff and nonsense," her mother was barely concealing her irritability.

Life from then on had been a joyless existence. Angela had been forbidden to write to Santa Claus, so, of course, she didn't get any special presents, only sensible ones from her parents, like mathematics sets and the complete works of Shakespeare. Gradually, her parents transformed her from a happy, normal little girl, into a mirror image of themselves – unforgiving, sarcastic, critical and – unhappy.

Angela's memories of her childhood were broken into by the sounds of heaving sobs coming from Enid the tea lady.

"You poor woman! Such deprivation! I'd like to give those parents of yours a piece of my mind!"

Angela smiled through her tears. There was no need. She had, in fact, already had her revenge. When her parents were both sixty five she had summoned *them*.

"You are both old now," she had said briskly, much in the manner that they had used towards her when she was seven. "And it is time that we all faced reality. You will undoubtedly have various health problems in the years to come. I'm a busy career woman and I don't have time to take care of you. So I've booked you both places at the Evening Sunset Retirement Home. You have two days to pack. You only need the essentials."

Her parents had meekly obeyed and moved themselves out of the family home and into a retirement facility. And, strange people that they were, Angela felt that they had done so with a sense of pride, taking comfort from the fact that they had raised their daughter to be as unemotional as they were.

In the back of The Christmas Shop, Terry Madeley felt distinctly uncomfortable. He was not used to children, having none of his own, and he found it very curious and unsettling that the contract for Living Lights should be decided by two teenagers. But that was what Mr Egan wanted and the customer was always right.

The Japanese boy, who was the inventor of the lights, kept quizzing Madeley about production capacities and quality control measures. It was quite unnerving, but he certainly seemed to know his stuff. There was no denying that the boy's questions were awkward, since Madeley had been forced to admit that his company, Egerton's, was technologically backward and, also, losing money. It looked as though the contract was going to slip through his fingers.

Nick had said little, up to that point, but he then tossed something into the conversation which made Madeley's business radar start pinging.

"Plinkbury is a very depressed area. People here don't have any jobs and they don't have any leisure activities. Would you consider setting up a new factory here?"

There was a silence. Egan patted Nick's head and Madeley's eyes glittered, as he frantically worked over the possibility in his head.

"Yes, yes I would," he answered, with a note of excitement in his voice. There was a lot to be said for setting up a new factory in a depressed area. There would be lots of available people to work in the factory, for a start, and they would probably be enthusiastic about new ideas - unlike the existing firm of Egertons, which had steadfastly refused to move with the times.

"Then I think we need to go and talk to the Council, don't you?" Egan smiled at Madeley. "Nick, go and fetch Christine. She should be in on this meeting."

At that moment, there was an unusually loud level of shouting from the square outside and all the shopkeepers came out to see what was happening. The Town Hall doors had been opened by an elderly lady wearing an apron and tinsel in her hair. Reporters and their crews rushed forward. Enid, the tea lady, held up a restraining hand.

"The Leader of the Council will make a statement very shortly. Please be patient," she said, in a very regal manner.

A groan of irritation went up from the media and they resigned themselves to hanging about in groups at the foot of the Town Hall steps.

Egan, Madeley, Nick, K and Christine, pushed through the crowds and went into the Town Hall. Egan took down the copy of the Royal Charter, as he passed, in case he needed to refer to it during the negotiations. The media enjoyed a little buzz of excitement. Whenever Egan was involved, things happened. Jane Hoffmeyer kept her eye on Christine. Before she wrapped up her final story on the Plinkbury protest, she was going to have another statement from that young girl. The news station had reported an overwhelmingly positive response in the US to young 'Christine Holiday' and her wise words about the spirit of Christmas.

In the Council Chamber, Angela Summer was now a remarkably cheerful woman. Years and years of loneliness and depression had come pouring out. Enid had kept her well supplied with strong, sweet tea throughout and Angela had astonished herself by the depths of her pent-up feelings. When she had finished crying buckets of tears and had been clasped to Enid's ample bosom, she felt like a great weight had been lifted from her soul. She had clung to Enid and the two of them had joined voices in a heartfelt rendition of *White Christmas*, to the accompaniment of the loudspeakers outside.

So when the handsome Egan, three teenagers and a sharp-suited businessman appeared in the Chamber, they were taken aback when Ms Summer greeted them with a smile and offered them seats.

Negotiations were remarkably quick and easy. Egan outlined the proposal that the Council should withdraw the ban on Christmas and, in return, Terry Madeley would build a new factory in Plinkbury to manufacture Living Lights. Egan also promised to make Plinkbury into The Christmas Capital of the World and put it on the tourist map. He threw a few statistics into the conversation, about how much his Valued Customers spent, all year round, on Christmas memorabilia. Angela Summer's eyebrows shot up and she beamed at him. Even Terry Madeley managed a rare smile, when he realised that he was definitely going to get the manufacturing contract.

So it was a serene and charming woman who stood on the Town Hall steps ready to issue a statement to the media. Everyone could see that Angela Summer had changed dramatically. They didn't know that her childhood had been brushed out of her mind, like a bad dream. Enid had told her magical stories of Christmas - as she had told her own children, many times. Enid believed, had *always* believed in Santa, ever since she had seen him, when she was young. Enid told the stunned Council Leader that, when she was just eight years old, she had crept down to the living room, in the middle of the night, just to look at the fairy lights on the Christmas tree. And she had seen Santa appear from the chimney and leave presents in the stockings hanging above the fireplace. She had watched him quite closely, she said, and she could remember every whisker on his dear face. She thought that she hadn't been seen but, as he turned to go back up the chimney, Santa had looked her right in the face and winked, before he disappeared in a puff of red, glittery dust.

"What about the Tooth Fairy?" Angela Summer had whispered to Enid.

"Oh my dear. Of *course* there's a Tooth Fairy! Why, all my children got money for every single one of their baby teeth and my Peter even had a tiny little note from the Tooth Fairy, telling him how nice and strong his teeth were! I've still got it at home."

So, the Angela Summer who stood on the Town Hall steps, was a woman who had taken magic back into her life and she was ready to give some of it to others. The loudspeakers were turned off and the crowded square subsided into a hush. All eyes were upon her.

"It is with much thought," she said, with a smile on her face, "and with regard to the wishes of the people of Plinkbury, who have clearly shown, over the last two days, that they wish to celebrate Christmas as fully as possible, that the Council has decided to revoke the regulations banning any Christmas displays in the town."

A huge cheer went up from the crowd. Still cameras flashed and movie cameras whirred.

"This is a complete about-face by the Council, Ms Summer. Was it public pressure that forced this change of heart?" asked one reporter, very loudly.

Ms. Summer paused for a moment, then she said. "No. It was not pressure – just the overwhelming presence of Christmas spirit."

"She never said a truer word," muttered Christine to Egan, "those chocolates are *really* strong."

"Mmm. We may have to modify them a little before we release them, in whatever form, to the general public." Egan was never one to abandon a good product.

"I also have another announcement!" Angela Summer raised her voice to silence the restless crowd. "Mr Madeley here, of Egerton Electronics, has, today, announced that he will be opening a new factory in Plinkbury, to manufacture the lights that you see on the Town Hall here. This will create six hundred new jobs."

An almighty roar went up from the crowd and, at the same time, Egan signalled to someone at the back of the square. Several guy ropes were pulled, and a huge, bare fir tree was hoisted upright, to stand at the back of the market.

The Living Lights quivered and shimmered on the Town Hall and then, as Christine and her friends had witnessed before, they shot from their positions on the building, like multi-coloured streaks of light, and fought amongst themselves to find some space on the fir tree. The crowd shrieked in astonishment as the lights flew over their heads, and then gasped in wonder as the lights settled down on the branches of the tree.

"Unbelievable," whispered Terry Madeley and a lump formed in his throat at the thought that he was actually going to manufacture such wonders.

Jane Hoffmeyer pushed through the media crush and sought out Christine. The cameraman was summoned.

"This is Jane Hoffmeyer, in the town of Plinkbury, England, where some amazing events have taken place today. This town has gone from having a total ban on anything Christmassy to hosting the ultimate celebration of Christmas – all in two short days. And I have here with me, young Christine Holiday, who was one of the original protestors against the Christmas ban and whose wise words, yesterday, touched the hearts of people around the world. So, Christine, what do you feel about the events in Plinkbury?"

Christine smiled. "I think that the last two days here have shown that people really carry the Christmas spirit in their hearts all year round and all they need is an excuse to bring it out. It's a shame that Christmas only happens once a year, because it would be nice if people were happy, kind and thoughtful every day. But, sometimes, life gets in the way, and people get down and frustrated. So, we should never ban the one time in the year when we can guarantee a good feeling, should we?"

Jane Hoffmeyer hardly heard Christine's words. She was too busy thinking about what she was going to win at next year's TV industry awards ceremony. This girl was outstanding in front of the camera!

Egan tapped Christine on the shoulder. "It's time for us to go," he whispered. Christine nodded.

Zazu said a tearful goodbye to Agnes but promised to return soon. Egan signed up Bella Shuttleworth and her husband as joint managers of the new Christmas Shop. The twenty percent staff discount on all goods purchased was enough to send Bella into a state of ecstasy. Egan reflected that she probably would have worked for nothing. Anyway, he left them in charge. "I have to go abroad on business," he said, "but I'll be back at the end of the week." There were contracts to be signed by Santa K and Egan was anxious to wrap everything up.

Egan finally got his chance to drive the Ferrari because it was daylight and they would need to travel by road until it got dark. As they pulled away from the square, the St.Nicholas market was in full swing once more. The loudspeakers were playing *Have Yourself a Merry Little Christmas*, and the shoppers were congregating around the huge decorated Christmas tree. And, with just a little touch of perfect magic, snow had begun to fall once more.

"Don't drop me off at the house," said Zazu, "I'm coming back to the conference with you. I've decided those Yule women need some beauty treatments before they go home for Christmas."

Christine agreed. She could see it would find favour with The Sisterhood. Even Ma Kringle had complained that the Finnish conference had no hairdressing facilities.

It was getting quite dark, so Egan pulled off the motorway and he and Nick changed places. Nick flipped the gear leaver into F and the car rose up into the star-studded sky.

"We'd better give the car a quick wash before we give it back to Babbo Natale," he observed, noticing that various market shoppers had spilt wine, ale and crumbs over the car, as they had passed it.

Everyone said that they would help – except Egan. After forty eight hours of wheeling and dealing and no sleep, he had finally crashed out in the back seat of the car and was snoring softly.

In Finland, the last news reports from Plinkbury were flashing up on the big screen in the conference hall. Everyone chuckled at the sight of the Christmas market in full swing, cheered when Angela Summer made her announcements, and fell silent with appreciation when Christine made her speech.

La Befana stood up and said softly,

"Mr Chairman, as the Emergency in England is now over, may I ask the conference to once more consider Kriss Kringle's proposal that the Yule Dynasty Gift Bringers be allowed to pass the job down to the female child, if there is no male heir."

The Chairman wiped his eyes, which had sentimentally pricked with tears during Christine's speech.

"Good idea," he said, in a muffled voice. "Kriss Kringle, would you read your proposal once more please?"

Pa Kringle stood and read the words.

"Those in favour, please raise their hands," the Chairman said.

One by one the hands went up, even Babbo Natale's and the Gift Bringers from China and Japan. Even Grandfather Frost from Russia put his hand up, although his mother, Babushka, had to prod him in the back first.

"And those against?"

Nothing. Not one hand. The Kringle proposal was through. Pa Kringle leapt to his feet and gave an almighty **"YAHOO!!!!"** which made several people jump. Ma Kringle rushed down from the wives' gallery and flung her arms around Pa.

"Just think Pa. In about a hundred years, our little Christine will be Santa Christine Kringle of the USA."

"Yep. They grow up so fast and you look back and wonder where the time went."

The End